WITCH HAPPENS

First edition. March 31, 2020.

Copyright © 2020 A. M. King.

ISBN: 978-1386751595

Written by A. M. King.

Thanks to my Father above for every blessing. Thank you to my wonderful family and readers for your support.

Witch Happens (The Summer Sisters Witch Cozy Mystery, Book 1)

Some people come from a long family line of lawyers, doctors, teachers and cops. Febe just found out she comes from a long line of...witches!

Febe Summer is not having a good day. Or a good year, for that matter. She lost her fiancé, her job, and her apartment all in one day—on her 25th birthday! Talk about the worst. Birthday. Ever!

She's jobless, penniless and soon to be...homeless.

Will she be able to rebound and pick herself up again?

Oh, and she just found out, thanks to a dark family secret, that she's not who she thought she was. She's a witch! And she's not allowed to practice magic—yet.

When she moves back to her small hometown of Blackshore Bay, there's more family drama than she can handle. Her aunties are out of control, her sister is being secretive and someone has murdered the malicious town gossip. Will she be able to find out who did it, before it's too late?

The Summer Sisters Witch Cozy Mystery series:
Witch Happens (Book 1)
Life's a Witch (Book 2)
Witch You Were Here (Book 3)

Chapter 1

"Women are angels. When someone breaks our wings, we simply continue to fly—on a broomstick. We're flexible like that."
–Author Unknown
-Febe's Favorite Quote of the Day

Febe Summer made her way up the steps of the subway station to the street level. Her pulse pounded hard in her throat. She needed to make it to the *Frutenac Comic* store by 8:30 a.m.

It was an overcast day with cloudy grey skies and the promise of rain to come. The gusts of wind blew her brunette curly hair into her face as orange and yellow leaves swirled around on the pavement on the ground.

She felt a tear in her stocking, but she would have to fix that later. She clutched her fall coat around her and her nametag slipped out of her pocket.

She picked it up and glanced at it. She hated the spelling of her full name, *February*. Her late mother had a thing about months and meanings. She was named after the Roman festival of purification called Februa where people were ritually washed. There was a Roman god called Februus. Her mom told her the month symbolized humility and sincerity.

But everybody called her *Febe*, pronounced *Feebee*. Thank the universe for that. Her sister was named after January, but in French: *Janvier*, meaning determined—and man did she live up to her name. And her other sister who was estranged from the family was named *Marsha*, a variation of March from Mars, the Roman god of war. Well, she was certainly at war with the family right now. Hadn't spoken to anyone since forever—or a few years to be precise.

Everybody used to poke fun at the Summer sisters in school because of that. She was used to being an outcast. Even at the ad agency. Some of the office bullies, and you know office bullies were everywhere these days, liked to point her name out. Jonathan was different, though. He would sit with her through lunch and they would go over ad campaigns together. In fact, he loved her creative ideas. She helped him out on a few of his campaigns, too.

It was 8:29 in the morning and she knew the store had to have opened. She'd made arrangements to meet the store owner, but she hoped her order would be ready. She had to zip back to the office pronto because she had a presentation at ten o'clock.

When she finally arrived outside the storefront on Acme Street near Yonge Street, she noticed Halloween decorations pasted up on the store windows: orange pumpkins, tall black hats, black cats, and a witch on her broomstick.

It was close to that time of the year again. Halloween. Everyone got their decorations up and merchandise out ready for spook fest and corporate costume parties. In fact, the office was having its own party next week.

Thankfully, the store had just opened and there wasn't a line. The last thing she needed was a line that would ruin her plans for the day.

Her mission had to be accomplished. She didn't have much time.

When she went up to the door her heart sank. It was closed.

Crap.

What's going on? He told me to be here at 8:30. I'm here. He's not.

She knew the store owner because being a bit of a comic nerd herself, she always collected the latest editions. Her boyfriend Jonathan was the same way. They had so much in common. She really lucked out meeting him. He was hot. He was everything she'd wanted in a guy. Caring *and* popular.

She meant to go the store as soon as it opened, grab the merchandise after she paid the balance, hop back on the subway, and bring it to Jonathan's apartment at the next subway stop at nine o'clock. Thankfully his condo building was right next to the Bay subway station.

Then back on the subway to make it to the office by 9:30. It was a good thing she had her metro pass so she wouldn't have to pay again. The plan was perfect. Only life was not. Things got into the way. Like a storeowner opening up his comic shop minutes late.

Time was everything. Every second counted, just like the person waiting for the bus. Each minute mattered. And like the Olympian sprinter, seconds counted. Well, right now, she timed herself to be back at the office and at her desk at precisely 9:30 a.m.. Jonathan's birthday was today and he worked at the same office as an account executive. Only he had to fly out to Vancouver for a conference, then fly back tonight. She wanted to surprise him before he flew out. He'd be leaving his condo to head to the airport at nine. She didn't want to miss him, but it looked as if she would.

Things were getting pretty serious between them. In fact, he'd unofficially proposed to her. He had a mountain of student debt and said when he cleared things up a bit, he'd buy her a ring she deserved. Still, it was the thought that counted.

She was still on probation at Harlington Advertising where she worked as a trainee account coordinator—the pay wasn't that fantastic but it helped cover the cost of studio apartment just west of Toronto on the subway line, the interest on her student debts, and food for her little kitty, Ebony, a black Bombay short-haired rescue cat with a muscular body and friendly temperament.

According to the animal shelter, black cats had the lowest adoption rate, yet they were known to be the gentlest and smartest. There was no member of the cat family that was so maligned like the black cat. For some reason, black cats carried the stigma of being revered, feared, witchy, or bad luck. Mostly in North America. In Europe it was good luck to have one, just as long as one never crossed your path, or so she'd heard.

Well, her baby crossed her path with a limp and mangled fur one day.

Ebony had apparently been badly abused by her previous owner, so Febe took her into her arms and took her home. She'd never looked back. Her kitty guarded her tiny apartment while she was out during the day, working long, politics-driven, caffeinated hours at the office.

She nervously glanced at her watch and the large red sign marked "Closed" in white block texts.

He'd promised that he would be there on time. She had to make it across town to the Agency. She couldn't afford to be late. Her boss, Amanda Harlington would kill her. Like, literally.

Amanda was not one to be trifled with. Her 88 year-old grandfather was the founder of the entire boutique agency which opened in the 1950 and had offices in Japan, Milan and New York. And Amanda was—well, she could be overbearing sometimes. Actually, all the time.

Still, Febe wanted to pick up the surprise for her boyfriend's birthday. They both shared the same birthday. She was stoked about how much they had in common. Even the same birthday. Imagine that!

When she'd first met him at work she knew it was her destiny. He'd started at Harlington just a year before she did. So he knew what it was like to be a newbie.

She was so thrilled to be going out with one of the up and coming executives—and to work with him. She'd been assigned on some tough campaigns with him.

She wondered what he saw in her. She was just an ordinary girl next door who liked to work extremely hard and who was far from perfect. Okay, like totally far from perfect, but had a knack for solving puzzles for clients.

She'd only been at the agency for five and half months out of her six month probation. She had a degree in liberal arts but could not for the life of her find work after graduation and the interest on her student loan wasn't going away soon. But things looked very hopeful—in her job and her love life. *Yay.*

Jonathan said that he wanted to start an agency of his own. Talk about ambition. And he wanted her to handle his client accounts for him.

Just then she saw something through the glass door. She saw a shadow move, then a man appeared. He had a Tim Horton's coffee in his hand and he walked up to the door, yawning, and flipped the red sign to "Open."

A sigh of relief escaped Febe's lips.

He then unlocked the door and opened it. The door chime sounded with a Count Dracula theme.

"Oh, thank God," she said to him.

He took a slurp of his coffee. "You're Febe right? Febe Summers?"

"Yes, I am. Sorry to sound rushy but I have to drop it off then head to work and you know, with rush hour and everything." She pulled out her purse and got her credit card ready to make the transaction.

"Oh, right." He sauntered behind the counter. "You ordered that first edition *Somicani* comic."

She walked in, her heels tapping on the hardwood floor of the store. "Yep, that's it. Please tell me it's here."

He yawned and took another loud slurp of his coffee. "I know you have to get to work, so I had everything prepared. It just came in late last night."

"Great."

"Now let me see." He pulled it out of its package and laid it on the table.

"Wow! Thank you so much. It's...beautiful." Well, in a vintage sort of way. It smelled of old paper and was yellowy but it was in a special display package from its previous collector.

"I hope your husband—"

"My fiancé," Febe corrected him.

But the sound of husband sounded so dreamy.

"Well, I hope your fiancé really appreciated what you went through to get this thing. It's one of a kind. Can't get it anywhere else."

Febe observed the wonderful artwork and the vintage feel of the comic book.

"This is going to cost you quite a fortune."

"I know. I'll put it on my credit card"

She knew that when she became a full-time staff member at Harlington, she'd more than cover the cost. This was so worth it.

"He said he's always dreamed of having the first edition of this comic. It's his favorite. He talked nonstop about how much his father tried to get it for him when he was younger, but they couldn't afford it at the time."

"Sweet. Well, I sure hope that he appreciates you and what you've done. It's quite expensive, not to mention the amount of time it took to get this."

"It *is* worth it. He's really a good guy."

The man scratched his head and sighed deeply. "I guess nice guys don't finish last after all."

"It's his birthday today. Actually, it's both of our birthdays."

"Sweet. Happy birthday."

"Thanks." Febe had just turned 25 today and Jonathan, 27.

They were supposed to celebrate their birthday together, but at least she would see him later that night.

"So here it is." He told her the price and Febe's jaw dropped open.

"Wow, that's a lot."

"Yeah, I know. But it also includes the overseas shipping charges."

"Of course."

Febe swiped her credit card and entered her PIN number.

"There you go ma'am." He handed her the carefully wrapped merchandise.

"Thank you so much."

Febe then looked at her watch and panicked.

She had to stop by Jonathan's condo and then zip across town back to the office to do her presentation. He would probably be gone by the time she got there, but she wanted him to see the comic as soon as he got back home. She was going to have to let herself in with the key he'd given her and place it on the counter by the doorway.

She didn't want him to miss his surprise. She couldn't wait to see the look on his face.

* * *

When she finally got up to his apartment, Febe drew in a deep sigh.

He had given her the key to his apartment in case of emergency and she never used until today. But she really wanted to surprise him.

She was going to place the comic on the countertop, since he'd probably already left for the airport. That way, when he came back home he would see his birthday surprise and she'd explain to him that she was able to get the first edition of his favorite comic after all.

She loved to surprise people close to her. It was one of her things. She'd done the same thing when her mother was alive. She'd wanted to see a baseball player, so when she was very ill,

Febe had asked his agent if it was possible and they'd made arrangements since he was in the area anyway. It had brought to tears of joys to her mother's eyes. She really missed her mom and could not believe she was really gone.

Febe turned the key in the lock and opened Jonathan's door.

She froze when she thought she heard the sound of someone struggling.

Her pulse pounded hard in her throat again.

My God, what's happening?

She reached into her pocket to call 9-1-1, but stopped. She slid the phone back in her satchel and grabbed a metal frame off the counter to arm herself against burglars.

He sounded as if he was in pain.

Was he in trouble?

She went to the room with the metal frame held firmly in her hand to strike whoever was attacking her fiancé.

But when she opened the door to his bedroom, her jaw fell open just as wide.

In bed was Febe's fiancé—with their boss, Amanda!

Chapter 2

Under the sheets, there he was. Jonathan, her fiancé with her boss, Amanda Harlington.

She kept playing the words over in her mind, still not processing it.

Seeing was *not* believing. Because what she saw, she did not believe. She had to be dreaming. No, she was having a freaking nightmare.

Her lungs squeezed tight, trying to suck in air. Dizziness and nausea swept through her body.

Talk about the wool over her eyes. She was blinded. By disappointment.

There she was, clutching a valuable historical comic for her boyfriend for his birthday.

"Febe! What are you doing here?"

"I came to surprise you...but instead, *you* surprised *me*!"

She looked helplessly from her boss to her boyfriend, back to her boss again.

He didn't even seem disappointed, or fearful, or embarrassed.

Damn it! Show me some remorse.

Jonathan just lay there under the cover as he rolled his eyes. "What are you doing here?" he asked again.

Oh my goodness he isn't even sorry?

"I'm here for your birthday? I thought you were already at the airport so I let myself in."

"Who the hell gave you the key?"

"*You* did."

"I'm sorry, Amanda," he said, turning to his boss, *their* boss, who still wore that dreadfully enormous diamond necklace around her neck. Did that woman *ever* take off that diamond necklace? It was as if she had to always rub her bling in everyone's face to let everyone know how super rich she was.

"I can explain everything," he said to Amanda.

"I can't believe you. I..." Febe was just too stunned to speak.

He then got up out of the bed. Their boss seemed to look inconvenienced and rolled her eyes.

Thankfully, he wasn't nude. He had his boxer shorts on. He walked out of the room and closed the door behind him.

"Listen, Febe," he sighed, "I'm sorry you had to find out this way but I was going to break it off with you."

Her heart stopped beating.

"Break it off with me—today?" Not that she wanted to be with that creepy cheat *now*. But the audacity to plan to break off with her today. After all she'd done for him.

"You do realize this is my birthday, right? And yours." She held the comic book in her hand.

"What's that?" he said and grabbed it from her. "Oh, man! This is the first edition. You got this for me? You shouldn't have!"

She took it back from him. "You're right. I shouldn't have. I'm going to donate this to a shelter."

"What? You crazy witch!"

She turned around, stunned. "What did you just call me?"

"A witch! All you women are the same. You just want to have your cake and eat it too. You think I wouldn't date other women?"

"We're supposed to be engaged. How could you?

"I was just saying that. Come on doll, you didn't really think we'd always be together. I mean look at you. Look at me. Come on. I don't need you to hold me back. I mean, with Amanda I can reach heights. Connections."

"What is that supposed to mean? When I was helping you with the orientation and with the ad campaign, you didn't think anything of it back then."

"That was different. This is now."

"I can't believe you. I can't believe I had the wool over my eyes this whole time."

"Wake up doll. You're just an average girl. You're nothing compared to Amanda. She's beautiful and perfect and has a lot of power and connections. She really knows how to move her way up in the world. And her granddaddy is the owner of the company. She's got everything. Hey, no hard feelings, eh?"

What?
No. Hard. Feelings?

Okay, so Amanda Harlington was perfect on the outside. Flawless smooth skin. Size 1 dress. Slim. Perfect hair with no split ends. Perfect make-up. And yeah, she was also twenty-five years old with a powerful position in the company, but that was because her granddad owned the joint. They had a lot of money. She probably grew up with governesses and trust funds.

Febe had none of that. She was the same age as Amanda and struggling to pay off student debts, had a bit of shape on her thighs, a little stomach bulge, and her hair wasn't perfect. Neither was her make-up. And she didn't wear designer clothes like Amanda. Her clothes were department store bargain section, sale-priced threads. Still, she was twice as nice as Amanda was. Not that being nice counted for much right now.

She didn't want to do something irrational. Her head was spinning. Amanda might be able to waltz into the Harlington offices at any time she chose because her granddaddy owned it, but Febe was still on probation. Amanda ran the show at Harlington Advertising. Staff members were terrified of her. Even her own grandfather feared her. She treated her granddaddy like a child! Amanda treated everyone as she pleased and there was nothing anyone could do about it.

Febe spun around on her heels and stormed out of his apartment, leaving the door open. He came to the door, but stood inside the doorway. He started to say something else but a gust of wind came out of nowhere and the door slammed hard while he was still talking.

That was weird.

Was there a sudden burst of wind in the building? Was there an open window somewhere? Jonathan hadn't closed the door.

She was too upset to think about it much, but she made her way to the exit door, swung it open, and practically flew down the stairs, taking two steps at a time. She didn't bother to wait for the elevator. Before she knew it, she was already down at street level.

She stomped down the street, her hair flying in the wind. Hustling through the busy morning rush-hour crowd on the sidewalk as she walked over to the subway station to get on the train to Bay Street.

While she sat on the train, she fought hard not to cry. She was better than that. She really needed to get a hold of herself.

He wasn't worth her tears. She could not believe how foolish she was. This morning, she'd thought everything was all right.

This was her worst birthday ever.

Thirty minutes later, she arrived at the Harlington glass office building on Bay Street.

"Good morning, Febe." The wonderful security guard said to her.

"Good morning, Sam."

"You all right this morning?" He said.

He was such a sweetheart, always saying good morning to her.

In fact, he always told her that she was the only executive there who actually acknowledged him as he stood guarding the main doors.

He appreciated that she spoke to him and treated him like a person, unlike some of the other executives who were too busy to know his name.

"I'm good, thank you," she said walking by his desk.

"Have a good day," she said.

Why should anyone else feel the brunt of her unhappiness? Mother always taught her to be polite and be kind to people and never take out your frustrations on others. She wished everyone at work was the same, but that was another story altogether.

Right now, she felt her world crashing down on her right now.

Where did she go wrong?

* * *

Febe grabbed a coffee from the Tim Horton's café near the elevator on the main floor.

Boy, she really needed her caffeine fix to jolt her awake for the day. She had to try hard to erase the horrible scene at Jonathan's apartment earlier. Get out of that frame of mind and step into a new frame of mind. She played over Katy Perry's upbeat pop tune *Roar* in her mind. She really needed that boost right now.

She pressed the button on the elevator to the eleventh floor.

When the double steel doors opened to her floor, she was greeted by the new company logo on the double glass doors across from the elevator.

Welcome to Harlington. Where magic happens.

Ha! That was her idea.

She came up with it during the company's brainstorming session as they were going through a major revamp of their image five months ago.

Well, she came up with the tagline, but Jonathan told the team about it. So *he* got the credit.

She was new at the time, her first week on the job...

Wait a minute.

Crap.

He took credit for her work. Gosh, how could she have been so blind?

He'd used her.

He told her that he mentioned her name to the big bosses, but no one ever came to her to tell her thanks. They just used it and the next thing she knew, *he* got the promotion to account exec from coordinator.

Double crap!

She took another dose of her delicious hot coffee.

She needed to brace herself for the day ahead. Amanda was supposed to be at that meeting later, so…

"Hey, Febe," Rebecca, the receptionist said.

"Hey, Rebecca. Any messages?"

"No, but I hear the boss is not too happy," she said in a low voice.

Febe's pulse hammered.

"Not too happy? Why?" Febe played naïve.

"Oh, she must've been at her boyfriend's place and they got stuck."

"Stuck?"

"Yeah, stuck in his apartment. Don't know who that guy is, but what a dud. How could he have jacked up doors like that?" Rebecca continued typing away at her computer while she spoke to Febe.

It was very clear to Febe that Rebecca and probably no one in the office knew that Amanda the boss was with Jonathan their co-worker. She didn't know if that was a good thing or a bad thing that no one suspected Amanda's affair.

"Wait a minute. Tell me more about the door."

"I don't know," Rebecca said, not looking up from her computer. "Something about the fire department had to go there and break the door down. It was jammed shut from the inside. Like somebody put crazy glue on the joints or something." She shrugged.

Febe's jaw fell open.

"Anyway, she did not sound too happy and said she might be a little late for the meeting, but to go ahead and start without her," Rebecca continued.

"I see. Got it. Um...thanks." Febe walked away from the reception desk, dazed.

What the heck just happened?

Her mind swirled back to the moments when she last saw Jonathan and she'd walked out of his apartment, then bam! The door slammed shut while he started to give her some sort of lame excuse and putdown about why he needed to be with someone better, like Amanda, who had connections, unlike poor little Febe.

Crap.

If she was being honest with herself, she *did* feel a weird feeling, a powerful wave of energy zap inside her body the moment before the door slammed shut.

She didn't think anything of it at the time. She'd just thought it was heartburn or stress or something. Or shock over what she'd witnessed. Her boss and her boyfriend—fiancé—in bed. Together. It was too much for her mind, right now. She took another chug of hot coffee.

She then glanced at her opened satchel handbag and sadness filled her heart.

Peeking out was part of the packaging from the comic book she'd bought him. She really should have just let him have it.

Nah, girl. You should've let him have it all right, but not the comic book, a swift whoop upside his head would have been good, a strange voice swept inside her mind.

What was that?

Was she going crazy all of a sudden?

She took a deep breath and sat down at her cubicle, taking her handbag off and placing it in the desk drawer beside her. Later, when she wasn't so angry, she'd give him the comic book. It was his present, after all.

Just then, Dave from the mail room and Rebecca the receptionist came to her desk.

"Is everything all right?"

"No, it isn't, Febe. We all have something we need to get off our chest," Rebecca said in a serious tone.

Next minute, a few more of her team members crowded around her desk.

"You think we didn't know?" Rebecca said, with her arms folded across her chest.

Febe's eyes opened wide. Oh, crap! Did they know about her and Jonathan? And now Amanda?

"Listen guys, I can explain..."

Before she could, they all broke into a wide grin and sang Happy Birthday.

Febe's blood pressure went down a bit. She could feel it.

"We knew it was your birthday, girl. Why didn't you say anything?" another co-worker said when they'd finished singing and handed Febe a large, creamy cupcake topped high with frosting and a single candle. That was the Harlington tradition to at least get a cupcake and a candle for whomever's birthday it was, unless it was one of the top dogs. They got a bit more.

"Thanks so much, guys. I...I'm speechless," she said. And she was. Good thing, she didn't start blurting everything out about Amanda and Jonathan. Not that it was anyone's business.

An hour later, Febe got ready for her meeting but was greeted instead by Amanda Harlington, who stood at the opening of her cubicle with her arms folded across her chest, her blond hair cascading down her shoulders, her manicured fingertips tapping on her sleeves.

"Hey, Amanda. I was just about to head to the boardroom."

"Well, you needn't bother."

"Why?"

"Because," she said, taking out a folder she had at her side. "Here is your evaluation. I don't think you've got what it takes to be here at Harlington. As you know, you're on probation and neither party has to give any notice if it's not working out. And truth be told, we need people like Jonathan, with creative talent."

Febe's eyes widened in shock. There was that feeling again inside her.

"What?"

She was seriously going to fire her on her birthday? Did this woman have no heart? She stole her fiancé, now she was stealing her joy?

Just then Sam the security guard, looking apologetic, came to escort Febe off the premises, as happened whenever anybody was let go.

Febe was too stunned to speak. Emotions climbed inside her. She was dazed. Shock.

"How could you?"

"I don't want to hear another word," Amanda said. "I'm sure you'll find something else more suitable for your skills."

Was Amanda afraid of Febe blurting to the whole company how she was sleeping with a subordinate, who happened to Febe's now ex-fiancé? Was that what this was really about? Febe was on probation, so technically, she didn't have much power to go to HR, even though she could fight it.

Febe shot up from her desk. "I don't need to work for someone like you," she said with what little pride she had left. She knew this was Amanda's company, her granddaddy's company.

There were some battles she should fight and some she shouldn't. She knew she would have to let the universe take over here. This was too big for her right now.

"And oh, happy birthday," Amanda said with a snarky tone.

Her co-workers looked as stunned as Febe did when she marched pass them with the security guard and a box with her belongings from her desk.

She could not believe she was having the worst birthday ever!

She no longer had a fiancé, she was penniless waiting for another paycheck that would never come, and now she was about to be homeless, too, because she could not afford to pay her rent.

Aside from waking up this morning, what the heck went wrong? This was a nightmare. It couldn't be happening.

She really needed to get a new life. It couldn't get any worse than that. Katy Perry's *Roar* started playing harder in her mind now. They hadn't seen the last of her—or had they?

Chapter 3

Later that evening, after walking around the city trying to figure things out, Febe stood in her kitchen getting Meow Mix for Ebony, her furry, four-legged baby. It looked as if they would *both* be eating cat food soon if she didn't find another job, pronto.

"Ebony, come here, baby."

Her beautiful black Bombay cat curled her soft tail around Febe's ankle which brought warm feelings inside her. Ebony was the only friend she could count on right now.

"Baby, it looks as if you and Mommy are going to have to find a cheaper place to live while I try to find a new job."

Her kitty purred gently and she scooped her up and hugged her close to her chest.

Ebony was a bit fussy, then Febe said, "Oops. I almost forgot your favorite tune."

Her little, black Bombay cat loved to listen to *Black Cat* by Janet Jackson. It was like her kitty's anthem. Funny thing was Ebony responded almost like a real person rather than a cat sometimes. Or maybe it was Febe's overactive imagination.

Febe touched the iPod and it came to life. The song crooned through the Bose sound dock system and Ebony started getting playful. It was the first time since morning that Febe smiled.

Just then her open laptop made a sound. It was an incoming call.

Crap.

She almost forgot her family was supposed to FaceTime her from Blackshore Bay to wish her a happy birthday. They usually did that around this time of the year. The women huddled on grandma's old sofa in that old Victorian house on the cliff where Febe had spent many memorable childhood summers. She wished she could go there and hang out, but she couldn't. They always acted a bit strange toward her.

Blackshore Bay would be the perfect place to regroup and take a much-needed stress-relief break from the big city. It was a cozy small town nestled near cottage country just an hour's drive north of Toronto.

Well, aren't you going to answer it? A voice inside her said.

Of course, I am, she answered back in her mind, thinking she really needed to take a break or she was going to go insane, talking to herself like that.

She sighed deeply.

As much as she didn't want to speak to anyone right now, she was always taught that friends could come and friends could go, but your family will *always* be your family.

She placed Ebony on the kitchen floor, went to her computer, and sat down on the couch.

"Hey," she said as cheerfully as she could after she pressed the accept call key.

"What in Sam's name is wrong with you?" Aunt Trixie said.

Aunt Trixie was the aunt who always spoke her mind. She was a spitfire in the family, but she was always there for her kin, no matter what.

"What?" Febe said, stunned.

"Trixie!" Aunt Eartha said, playfully tapping Aunt Trixie's arm. "It's the girl's birthday. Have some manners."

Aunt Eartha was like Mother Earth. Motherly, loving, always there. She was the wise one of her aunties.

"Sorry, darling," Aunt Eartha said, apologizing on her little sister's behalf. "How are you by the way? Happy blessed birthday!"

"Thank you, Aunties, and no worries."

"Vannie, are you coming?" Aunt Trixie called out.

"Yes, yes, I'm here. I'm coming."

Her Aunt Vanity, whose real name was Vanessa but everyone called her Vanity because seriously, she was always into herself. Always had a mirror, obsessed with her looks, her status and how everyone else saw her.

"Happy Birthday to you. Happy Birthday to you. Happy twenty-fifth birthday. Happy Birthday to you," they sang out of tune so badly, it almost gave Febe a warm, sentimental smile. Well, at least something was back to normal in her life.

Her late mother's older sisters Aunt Eartha, Aunt Trixie and Aunt Vanity were each there singing their dear hearts out. Bless them.

"Thank you," Febe said and burst into tears.

"Hey, what's wrong sweetie," Aunt Eartha said soothingly. "I'm sorry it wasn't in tune, you know how..."

Febe shook her head and waved them on. "No. No it's not that." She couldn't contain her emotions any longer.

Heck, if she couldn't be herself around family, what was the point?

"I lost my job and my fiancé today, and I'm going to lose this apartment."

They froze.

She dabbed her eyes with a tissue from the box on the side table while she sat, legs folded, opposite the laptop on her coffee table. Ebony was busy nibbling on her treats in her kitty bowl.

When she looked back up at the computer screen, she saw them all huddled around the computer with looks of shock and pity on their faces. It was the first time she saw them speechless. Really speechless.

Then when she peered closer, she realized they weren't saying anything or moving. She leaned closer. What was happening?

Then she realized the computer screen had frozen.

Crap.

She pressed on a key and another one but nothing happened for a moment. Just then Ebony, who had finished her kitty meal, strutted across the table and curled up on Febe's lap.

The moment that happened, the computer screen unfroze and they were talking.

"What happened?" she asked.

"You froze on us, girl," Aunt Trixie said.

"You froze on me, too."

"Anyway, Febe, I'm not sure if you caught what I said earlier but we're so sorry this all happened on your birthday," Aunt Eartha offered.

"Would it have made a difference if it happened any other day?" Aunt Trixie said, sarcastically.

Aunt Eartha rolled her eyes at Aunt Trixie, while Aunt Vanity seemed oblivious to the whole situation.

Aunt Vanity was looking into her compact mirror, touching up her bottle-blond hairdo. Febe remembered how traumatized Aunt Vanity got when she found her first gray hair. Ever since, she swore she'd never be gray again—in that Scarlett O'Hara way, like at the end of *Gone with the Wind*, Scarlett swore she'd never go hungry again. Aunt Vanity could be such a drama queen sometimes.

"You know what I meant, Trixie. You know what I meant, don't you darling niece?" Aunt Eartha's voice was filled with genuine concern. "Darling, what happened?"

Febe was suddenly glad that her sister Janvier wasn't there to watch this. She was usually at the old Victorian house with their aunties since moving back to Blackshore Bay, but she'd already texted Febe and told her that she would be working late at the family's Summer Café and wished her a happy birthday already. If only she knew how *unhappy* it was...

"Well," Febe sniffled, trying to gain her composure. "First, it started off with..."

"Vanity, pay attention," Aunt Trixie said while Aunt Vanity started to powder her face. She was always powdering her face. Febe was sure someone had put a hex on her auntie so she'd be glued to a mirror—not that she believed in witchcraft.

"Huh." Aunt Vanity looked embarrassed. Even though she was seated on the sofa turned to the side, she didn't realize that she was in view of the camera.

"Pay attention. Don't you see the girl's trying to tell us about her pitiful birthday?"

Well, that made Febe feel more confident.

"Yes, yes. I'm listening. She lost her boyfriend or something, right? Did she find him?"

Aunt Trixie rolled her eyes. "Sorry, Febe. What were you saying?"

"I was just saying that." Febe knew how protective her aunties were of her and her sisters, especially since their mother had died last year. They could drive her up the wall sometimes, but they'd drive a steak knife into anyone who dared mess with them. So Febe decided to tell a condensed version.

"He just broke it off with me."

"What? That scoundrel."

"I'm so sorry to hear that, Febe. And on your birthday? He knew it was your birthday, right?"

Febe nodded slowly and dabbed her eyes again. She knew he wasn't worth the tears but she just couldn't help herself. It wasn't that she was crying over him as much as she wanted to rid herself of any emotions attached to him.

Crying was cleansing, she'd once read somewhere.

"What a waste," Aunt Trixie said, her arms folded tightly across her chest.

"Excuse me?" Febe asked, confused.

"What a waste. Instead of spending your time wiping away your *tears*, you need to spend time wiping away *the people* that caused you to shed a tear in the first place," Aunt Trixie said. "I've got a spell I can cast on him, if you want."

Febe didn't quite get the last part of her aunt's sentence about a spell and thought maybe she heard wrong or Aunt Trixie was up to her tricks again, telling her crazy jokes.

"Trixie Summers!" Aunt Eartha scolded with shock. "Do *not* give the girl such nonsense advice. And you will not be casting spells on anyone!"

"What? She should just forgive him and forget what happened?" Aunt Trixie shot back.

"Forgive and *move on*. Forgiveness is not for *him*. It's for *her*. She needs to release toxic feelings about him. You know they only serve to hurt the holder of the feelings, not the target. Never let anyone who's not worthy of your priceless, precious time on Earth take up any room in your thoughts. You need good thoughts to get ahead. Time spent on getting even is time wasted for getting ahead. Toxic feelings are harmful feelings," Aunt Eartha finished.

"Not to mention what it does to your pores. All those toxic emotions seeping through you." Aunt Vanity glanced into her compact mirror, looking at her cheekbones, touching her face with her free hand.

Febe wanted to break out into a grin at her Auntie's non-stop self-concern.

"That's not all," Febe said.

"Yes, dear. You were telling us about your job."

"Yeah, I...I didn't make it to the end of the probationary period." Febe bit down on her lower lip.

She didn't want to excite them too much. It would just make her feel worse, not better. She'd tell them another day. But not now. Besides, she was feeling bad enough about her twenty-fifth birthday.

"What? How come?" Aunt Eartha said. "I thought you were doing so well. All those wonderful campaign logos you were coming up with."

"I know," Febe said quietly. "It just wasn't working out, okay? I'll explain more another day. I'm too tired to go into it all right now."

"Oh dear. Okay, sweetie. But what about your apartment. Do you need money?"

"Sis, you know we're broke, right?" Aunt Trixie arched her brow and leaned toward her older sister.

Aunt Eartha sighed deeply. "No, we're not quite broke, Trixie."

"I'd hardly call being house rich and cash poor, a windfall, dear."

"Trixie! Do you mind?"

"Fine."

"Sorry, darling," Aunt Eartha turned back to the screen to speak back to Febe. "Now what makes you think you're going to lose your apartment?"

"I...I was counting on getting a raise once my probation was over in a couple weeks in time to pay the next installment on my rent. I already used up my savings as it is. Toronto's not the cheapest city in the world to live."

"I hear you, girl," Aunt Vanity said, still fixing herself up in her small vanity mirror. She was trying on a new shade of lipstick. It was unreal. "I used to live on the lake in the downtown core, remember? The theatre district?"

"Oh, yeah, right."

"Anyway, you should move back to Blackshore Bay, darling," Aunt Vanity said, not looking into the computer.

"Actually, she's right," Aunt Eartha agreed.

"Where's she gonna stay? I'm not sleeping on the sofa," Aunt Trixie teased.

"No one is sleeping on any sofa, Trixie dear. This mansion that was left to us by our dear grandmother has plenty of room. She can have her mother's old room. Janvier is already in there."

"The two of them, together?" Aunt Trixie arched her brow.

"For now, until we get the spare room set up. Anyway," Aunt Eartha said turning back to the screen, "you can come here and stay with us and work at the Summer Café. We always need an extra hand there."

"Are you sure, Aunt Eartha?"

"You worked there one summer before, remember?"

"Yeah, when Mom was alive. She really wanted me, Janvier, and Marsha to work in the family business."

"Yes, I know, darling. That was her dream."

"Well, I'd told her that I wanted to live in the city and work in advertising after my degree, but..."

"But what?"

"I'm a total failure, let's face it," Febe blew out a puff of air.

"Well, nobody's perfect," Aunt Trixie said.

"Trixie!" Aunt Eartha chastised. "Sorry, sweetie. Listen, and listen to me good. If you haven't gone through life without any blemishes, upsets, letdowns, disappointments or pain, then you haven't lived, got that?"

"Whoa. I guess you're right."

"I know I'm right darling," Aunt Eartha said. She then exchanged glances with Aunt Trixie and looked back at the screen. She could hear Aunt Vanity whisper something like, *aren't you going to tell her?*

"Sweetie," Aunt Eartha finally said."

"Yes, Auntie?"

"Um...have you been having any strange feelings, lately?"

"Strange feelings? Depends. Like what do you mean?"

"Well, any weird energy levels? Or anything strange happening to you, especially today?"

All three ladies leaned forward with their right ear directed to the screen of the computer camera as if waiting for her response.

"Um. No." Just then Ebony's ears stretched up. She started to hiss and Febe felt another strange sensation.

"Hey, wait a minute," Febe said, "Come to think of it. I did. Today."

"What was it dear?" Aunt Eartha asked, concerned.

"Well, I...um, thought something strange happened today at Jonathan's apartment."

"Like what?"

"When we were arguing, I left and stood outside the door. He stood inside his apartment and started to ramble something insane that really got under my skin. I got angry. I could feel my temperature rise, then it was like there was a swift burst of wind or weird electrical energy that just zapped through me or around me and the next thing I knew, the door slammed hard in his face. I didn't think anything of it at the time, but it was really weird. I felt so, so *drained* afterward, like I'd just ran a marathon without sleep or something. And then later...I found out that he was locked in his apartment for a while."

Febe watched as their eyes widened with shock.

Well, Aunt Vanity was still fixing her hair looking in the mirror in her hand.

They exchanged funny glances with each other and said nothing for a moment.

"Darling," Aunt Eartha finally said, "there's something we need to talk to you about." Her tone was more serious this time.

Febe's heart thumped hard in her chest. "W-what? What is it?"

Febe had a sinking feeling that she really didn't want to know.

"Well, how should we say this?" Aunt Eartha chewed on her lower lip. That wasn't like her. She only did that when she was super nervous and she wasn't usually. Not these days. "You've come of age, Febe."

"Of what?" Febe arched her brow, dubiously.

She thought she'd come of age when she turned *eighteen*. Was Aunt Eartha feeling all right? Febe was *long* past coming of age.

"In our family, there is...well, something that is not shared with anyone. We had this discussion with your sister, Janvier, when she turned twenty-five two years ago and then she came here to live with us. We won't be speaking to your sister Marsha until she comes of age which is another year or so."

"What is it?"

They each exchanged funny glances again.

"You're not normal, honey," Aunt Trixie blurted out.

"What?" Febe said stunned.

"Trixie!" Aunt Eartha shouted, angry. "Do you know anything about breaking something gently to someone?"

"Nah!" Aunt Trixie just folded her arms across her chest with her chin up.

Aunt Eartha took a deep breath and sighed deeply. "Sorry, darling."

"What does Aunt Trixie mean by that?" Febe asked, suspiciously.

"It's just that...well, it's time we had this talk."

"What talk? Please tell me it's not about *sex*."

"More like *hex*, darling?" Aunt Trixie said, grinning widely.

Aunt Eartha gave Trixie the *look*. She then turned her attention back to Febe.

Aunt Eartha then cleared her throat. "What she meant to say, sweetie, is that..."

Aunt Trixie leaned forward and blurted out, "You're a witch!"

Chapter 4

"What?" Febe's jaw fell open.

Did her auntie just call her a witch?

That was the second person who'd told her that today. And her ex-fiancé was being a jerk when he called her that.

But her aunties were not being jerks. They were serious. But this couldn't be. She must have heard wrong. She searched their faces while staring in horror at the computer screen for any sign that she could have possibly heard wrong.

"Did you just call me a witch?" Febe finally blurted out, unable to control herself, as insane as the word *witch* sounded coming from her own lips.

"Well..." Aunt Eartha looked uncomfortable and cast a sideways glare at Aunt Trixie before looking into the computer camera. "What she meant to say, sweetie, is that..."

"You came from a long line of witches," Aunt Trixie interjected.

"Trixie!" Aunt Eartha said.

"What?" Aunt Trixie feigned innocence. "It's *true*. Why are you going to sugar coat it? It is what it is. You know I'm always one to speak my mind, right?"

"Too much," Aunt Eartha said.

"Aunt Eartha," Febe said, dazed, "none of this makes any sense to me."

"It will when we see you, dear. It's better that we speak in person. We were hoping you'd be here with us when you had your...coming of age, but we understood that you had work obligations."

"I see. So that's why you were trying to get me to be there for my birthday, in Blackshore Bay?"

"Yes, darling." Aunt Eartha exhaled sharply.

"Are you trying to tell me that we're all witches? Even Janvier?"

"Yes and no."

"Yes and no?"

"Well, yes, we have the gene."

"The gene? What gene?"

"The magical gene, darling."

Febe stared at her computer screen in horror. She could see her aunties hovered over their computer. Well, Aunt Vanity was busy filing her nails now. Ebony crawled off Febe's lap and went to take a nap in her kitty basket by the electric fireplace near the TV. She curled up and fell asleep as if she had not a care in the world. Right now, Febe wished she had no cares in the world.

This morning, everything seemed so normal. She had a good job, a way to pay off her debts, a cozy apartment on the subway line near her job, a fiancé and a normal family that acted crazy at times.

Now, she had no job, no way out financially, no apartment as of next month and she'd just found out her family members were witches.

Some people came from a long family line of lawyers or doctors or accountants or police officers...why oh, why did she have to come from a long line of witches? Was that even possible?

She took a deep breath and exhaled slowly.

"Okay, let me get this straight," she said, looking into the computer screen again. "We're from a long line of witches? Even my... mother?" She felt squeamish saying that. But she had to know the truth. As strange as everything sounded to her, for some reason it seemed to resonate inside her, and she found that very thought disturbing.

"Yes, darling," Aunt Eartha said, calmly.

"Unbelievable," Febe said, grabbing a chunk of hair in her hand.

"Yes it is, isn't it? Your sister Janvier had trouble with it at first, too, when we first told her on her twenty-fifth birthday."

"Okay, whoa. Wait a minute. What's this about twenty-fifth birthdays?"

"It's a lot to go into dear. When we see you, we'll explain everything and there's more for you to see."

"There's more?" She arched her brow.

"Yes. You see, Blackshore Bay is a small town, not really on the map, and there's a reason why."

"Why's that? Don't tell me because everybody's a witch there?"

"No, no darling. Don't be silly."

"Don't be silly? You just told me that we're all witches—women dressed in black that fly on broomsticks."

Aunt Trixie squirmed on her seat. "Oh, dear God. Please do not say that!"

"Say what?"

"The stereotypes, darling," Aunt Eartha interjected.

"What stereotypes?" Febe was lost now. If she wasn't lost before, she was certainly lost now.

"The stereotypes of witches. We've come a long way from the Salem Witch Trials but Trixie and I are on The Council's Voluntary Board for Advancement of People with Magic."

Febe reached over to the side table and grabbed the bottle of wine that was supposed to have been for her birthday dinner, looking dazedly at the screen. She poured herself a glass and took a swig.

"You can't be serious," Febe said slowly a moment later.

Aunt Eartha and Aunt Trixie exchanged funny glances again then looked back at the FaceTime screen. "Yes. We are serious, darling. When you come back here, everything will make sense."

"No disrespect, Auntie, but I *seriously* doubt that."

"Anyway, darling," Aunt Eartha continued. "For centuries our people have fought to eliminate these harsh negative stereotypes against our people."

"What harsh stereotypes? Witches on broomsticks, cackling in their long black hats...?"

"Uuuuurgh!" Aunt Trixie shrieked again, this time covering her ears with her hands.

"Darling, those are horrible stereotypes and only makes things harder on us," Aunt Eartha interjected. "We need to fight it, but we certainly can't have members of our family accepting those. Do *we* really look like that or behave like that?"

"Well, no. Of course not."

"Did your *mother* look like that or behave like that?"

"Of course not." But then again, she still wasn't convinced that her mother was a witch. Her mother was beautiful and had long, flowing ebony hair. Her skin was soft and glowing and her voice as soothing and kind as her heart.. People always told her mother that she was a dead ringer for Catherine Zeta-Jones, the Hollywood actress. Now, sadly her mother was no longer with them.

"Do we behave in such a hideous manner wearing long black cloaks, tall black hats, cackling at the moon?"

Febe grinned with embarrassment. "Well. No."

"Then please don't hurt the cause by buying into that negative stereotype that only seeks to keep us all down as a group. We are not like that in reality. It's the media's perception about us."

"It is?" Febe arched her brow.

"Yes. And I've been fighting to get this Halloween business straight."

"What? What do you mean? I thought witches *loved* Halloween. Not that I thought witches really existed."

Aunt Trixie cringed again. "Oh, pull-ease! Are you crazy, girl? No self-respecting witch would buy into that negative hype. It makes us all look crazy and evil, riding on broomsticks, wreaking havoc. Who ever heard of such a thing?"

"But...how do you...get around?"

"The same way you do, silly." Aunt Trixie was not amused.

"Some of us do get around on stick, dear," Aunt Vanity added. "Depends on the type of stick, of course."

"But not those horrible *old* broomsticks. Do you really think those things could fly with all the magic in the world?"

"Trixie! Be kind to the girl." Aunt Eartha was her usual protective self with Febe, for which she was grateful. This was all a lot to sink in, especially on her birthday. Not that if she'd found out on any other day, it would have made a difference.

"Well, actually, it's not entirely true," Aunt Vanity said, still filing intently on her long, manicured fingernails. "You see we can levitate and move swiftly to get around. Some of us, anyway," she said.

"Oh, I see."

"No, you haven't seen anything yet, but you will darling," Aunt Trixie said.

"But be warned, you are experiencing things now, like magical feelings, intense energies, but you will not be able to practice magic fully until you become licensed."

"What? Licensed? For what?"

"To practice magic, darling. Just because certain people might be able to drive, doesn't mean they should drive on the road unless they've been tested and learned the proper rules of the road. I'm sure any idiot can get into a car and switch on the engine and steer it on the road. Or take something like healing. That's more in line with the craft."

"The craft?"

"Yes, dear. The craft. Anyway, most people know how to nurse a wound but you need a license to call yourself a nurse or to practice in a safe manner with the public. Magic is similar. It's all in the handbook we have for you."

Febe took another swig of her drink. "Okay, now I know I'm going insane. This is all a dream. I'm going to wake up soon and this will all be over like...puff."

"No, darling. I'm afraid it's real. Very real. We'll have you registered with the Council of Witches in no time."

"The *Council* of *Witches*? There's a council for this thing?"

"Yes, it's like a secret society around here. We'll explain more later, dear. Madam Techer will be your teacher. You'll be taking classes with her soon to study for your license."

Febe took another swig of her drink, trying to drown out the truth or soak it all in without getting sick. "So I'll have to go back to school, after I've just finished uni?"

"Yes. But as you know, in life, you never stop learning. You can't know it all. Every day we learn something new."

"You're telling me," Febe said with a glazed expression.

"But you must be careful. Not everyone knows about us or wants us around. There are certain elements of society that would rather we didn't exist. Now the Bay is a safe town for us, but it's a magic-free zone. We can only practise or use our powers when it is very necessary and only in certain controlled environments."

"Or what? We'd have our license *revoked*?" Febe arched her brow, trying hard not to grin.

"Worse than that, dear."

The smile was wiped off Febe's face.

Chapter 5

Twenty minutes later, her FaceTime session ended with her aunties, Febe shook her head as she got off the sofa .

Her mind was still in a daze. She went into the kitchen to grab a cup of coffee, then changed her mind.

What she probably needed was another glass of wine. She'd planned to share her bottle of wine with Jonathan, after they'd both celebrated their birthdays when he got back from Vancouver. But that didn't happen, did it? In fact, nothing in her day went as planned.

What was wrong with her life? Like, seriously.

She would need to pack soon. She'd already paid her rent for the month of October and the landlord could keep the last month's rent deposit if he had a problem with her not giving him much notice. She would totally understand that. Right now she had other things bubbling in her brain.

"Can you believe that, Ebony?" Febe said, talking to her now woken black cat. Ebony was stretching and yawning. Not that she'd had a long nap.

"I'm a...a witch," Febe said breathless.

"I know, right?"

Febe placed a few dishes into the dishwasher and closed the door and pressed the start cycle. "I mean, imagine that. I can't..."

Febe froze.

She then spun around in shock. Eyes widened as if she'd seen a ghost. Her heart fluttered in her chest.

Okay, keep calm, Febe. You're hearing things. You're simply hearing things, that's all. Keep calm and grab a coffee.

"D-did...did you just...t-talk?" She said to her cat.

Ebony yawned again, not a care in the world as she sat in her kitty basket.

Phew, I thought for a minute I was going crazy.

"No, you're not going crazy, girl," Ebony spoke again. "I'm really quite glad you finally got it together and you've come of age. It was a drag waiting for this moment. Do you know how crazy it is to keep your mouth shut and pretend you don't have a voice? You have *no* idea."

Um. Okay. Now it's safe to panic.

Febe felt faint. She immediately flopped down on the kitchen island stool and arched her brow, her jaw still hung wide open.

"W-what did you j-just say?"

Her black cat was possessed.

"W-who a-are you?" Febe asked, cautiously.

"Oh, no, girlfriend. Please do not be afraid. I'm just a friend."

"B-but. It's impossible. You're the cat I...I rescued from..."

"Hmmm-mmm. Yeah, sorry about that, girl. It was all part of the plan. It was a test. Well, the first part anyway."

Febe thought she was really losing her mind now. "Excuse me?"

"You see, I crossed your path on purpose, limping and all. It was all part of the plan to see what kind of heart you had, to see if you deserved to have me around, protecting you and all. You aced that test."

"What?"

"Nothing's a coincidence, doll. Don't let the universe fool you. Sometimes things happen because they were supposed to happen. You wouldn't have scooped me up and kept me with you if I hadn't crossed your path that day."

"What makes you say that?"

"Come on now girl, you had your studies, your job. Your life was way too busy to have me around. You weren't even planning on having a family of your own until you reached your thirties."

"Hey! How did you know?"

Febe scratched her head, still dazed that her *cat* was speaking to her.

Then a flood of embarrassment washed over her. All this time, she thought Ebony was just a cat.

What about those embarrassing private moments?

Crap.

Febe spoke to herself a lot, didn't she?

Double crap.

Ebony probably overheard her talking about her most private thoughts and feelings. She would have kept her mouth shut if she had known her kitty understood every single word and would one day talk back to her. She couldn't afford to let Ebony out of her sight now. She knew too much about her, she half-joked in her mind.

Febe drew in a deep breath. This was not going to be easy.

Chapter 6

Later that night, Febe finished her shower and got ready for bed. Still in shock, her mind was spinning with disbelief over the events that had unfolded during the day.

She was a witch.

Her black Bombay cat, Ebony could talk. And oh, boy could she talk.

Her aunties were all witches, too. So was her sister, Janvier, and her late mother.

Okay, this was too much for her brain.

Too much information. Too much to process too soon. This was by far the worst. Birthday. Ever!

As she toweled off her hair, Ebony strutted into the room. Whereas in the past she would undress, talk to herself, or whatever when Ebony was around, now, she was way too self-conscious.

"Um, excuse me, Ebony," she said, feeling deeply uneasy about how to approach this without offending her black Bombay. "I'm about to...get ready for bed." She didn't want to pull off her robe and expose her bare skin in front of Ebony—not anymore.

"Oh, excuse me," Ebony said, "You didn't mind having me in the room all the other times."

"Yes, but..."

Okay, this was too insane. She was speaking to her cat *and* her cat was speaking back to *her*.

"You weren't talking then," Febe finished her sentence.

"Oh, I get it. You didn't mind doing whatever the heck you pleased when I was in the room because I was just your dumb cat."

"No!" Febe's voice raised an octave. "No, no, no. Of course not. Ebony, you know I would *never* look at you that way."

"When I said *dumb* cat, I'm not referring to the informal definition of a having reduced intellectual capacity, darling. I'm referring to the formal definition of one who is unable to *speak*," Ebony said, suddenly sounding more like a British-accented professor, than a casually-speaking cat.

Okay. "Um, listen. I get it...I just...listen all of this is new to me, okay. I've got to figure out my life now."

"Oh, darling, I'm just pulling your leg. You'll have to get used to my wry sense of humor."

Febe gave her a startled look. "I don't think your wry sense of humor is my biggest concern right now, Ebony."

"Right, of course," she giggled.

It was so bizarre watching her cat giggle like that, her little black tummy jiggling.

Just then her cell phone rang, startling her.

She went over to the bedside table to answer it.

She glanced at the screen. It was her sister, Janvier.

Why would Janvier be calling her now?

They weren't exactly close or anything. In fact, Janvier had always been evasive when it came to talking about the family or anything else, for that matter. Whenever she did speak to Febe, Janvier preferred to text or send an email, even if she were in the same house. Granted Grandma Summer's massive Victorian house could easily house five families. There were so many quarters and hidden passageways. It was creepy and massive. One would hardly go from one end to the other to speak to someone.

"Hey, Jan," she finally answered cautiously.

"Hey, Sis. Happy Birthday again," Janvier sounded unusually bubbly. That was so unlike her. Was this whole world turned upside down or something? "Did you get my text earlier?"

"Yeah, I did. Thanks so much. I replied with a thumbs-up emoticon."

"Ah, yeah. Of course." There was silence on the phone line for a moment. "Listen, I just spoke to Aunt Trixie."

"Oh." She knew there was a reason for Janvier calling.

"I know you have a lot on your mind right now. I did, too."

"I can imagine. Why didn't you tell me this before?"

"The same reason why I couldn't speak to you before and the same reason everyone has been a bit standoffish with you since you turned eighteen."

"What? Why?"

"Listen, chick. I'm coming to get you. I just got off the highway. I'll be there in a moment. We'll drive back to Blackshore Bay together okay?"

"Um. All right. But are you sure?"

"Yes, I'm sure."

"But I need time to pack."

"No worries, Sis. I'll help you."

"Okay, now I'm really suspicious."

"Why?"

"Because you are never nice to me. Not unless there's a hidden reason."

There was silence on the phone.

"Actually, Sis. You're intuition is getting sharper."

"What do you mean by that?"

"I'm coming to kill you."

Chapter 7

"Did you just say you're coming to *kill* me?" Febe asked her sister over the phone, not believing what she'd just heard. "And you expect me to stay here waiting for my demise?"

There was silence on the other end of the phone line. All she could hear was the sound of traffic and wind blowing.

Janvier was driving with the window open.

Dead air. Then that funny beep as if someone had hung up their cell phone.

Febe stared into the phone with shock.

Was her sister up to her old prankish tricks again? This wasn't funny. Not one little bit.

"What's up, girl? Cat got your tongue?" Ebony said.

"What?" Febe turned to Ebony, stunned.

"Sorry, couldn't resist. That saying came from the Middle Ages. It was thought that if you saw a witch, her cat would steal or control your tongue such that you could not report the sighting. Never did like that saying, anyway."

"Yeah, well, I'm not sure what to feel right now." She slumped down on her bed, dazed. "I never could read my sister."

"What's going on?"

Suddenly, as weird as it sounded, Febe was glad she had someone to talk to right now. In the city, everybody was preoccupied with their smartphones, dealing with the pressures of work. No one really interacted much.

"Did you hear my phone conversation, Ebony?"

"I heard it, girl. Don't worry. I'm here in your life for a reason. There's a reason evil people fear cats, especially black cats."

Suddenly, Febe was glad her black cat could talk. She had a true, loyal friend.

There was a loud pounding on her front door. Her heart knocked hard against her ribcage.

Who was that?

She glanced at the clock then went over to the door and peeked through the peephole. She saw no one.

"Who is it?"

"Your sister, Jan."

"Go ahead, girl, answer it. She's straight," Ebony said walking past the door.

"Right. Of course." Cats were good at sensing evil. It was obvious her little guardian was there looking out for her and didn't sense any fear.

She slowly opened the door leaving the chain on, just to be sure. She'd read about people being morphed into other beings from those comics she loved reading.

"Hey," Janvier said. "I'm good." Janvier stood there with her dark brunette hair up in a ponytail. She must have just finished work at the café. She always wore it down on days she was not working around food.

Febe unhooked the chain and opened the door wider, staring at her suspiciously.

"What?" Janvier said.

"What do you mean what? You scared the crap out of me just now."

"Oh, that. Sorry, Sis," she said, walking through the apartment, looking around. "I didn't mean to terrorize you just now. Just having a little fun. You know it's good to have a sense of humor."

"Yeah, if it's tasteful."

"Hey, Eb. What's going?" Janvier turned to Febe's black cat.

"Not bad. Yourself?"

"Trying to keep it real."

"I hear you." Ebony then waltzed into the bedroom leaving the two sisters alone, Febe with her jaw wide open in shock.

"You know my cat can talk?" Did everyone know about Febe's life, except her? Why was she always the last to know everything?

"Relax, Sis," Janvier rolled her eyes. "We all knew."

"You did?"

"Who do you think sent her here to watch over you while you were at university and living in the big city all by yourself?"

"What?"

"You know Aunt Trixie doesn't mess around, right? She's one crazy cat lady."

"So she sent Ebony?"

Janvier shrugged. "Kind of. You got anything to drink?"

"Um. Yeah, what do you want? Hot or cold?"

"I could use a coffee right now."

"Aren't you worried about being up all night?"

"I don't think either of us will be sleeping tonight, Sis."

"Oh, great."

Janvier helped herself to the coffee maker.

"Anyway, sorry about earlier. We got cut off. Bad reception under the bridge. But when I said I'm going to kill you, I meant

I'm going to kill that weak person Febe used to be. She's dead now. Gone. She's no longer a woman, she's a witch. You've come of age, Sis. Congratulations."

"Yeah, well, I don't know what to say about that. I don't feel as if it's anything to celebrate if you know what I mean."

"Hey, it's no worries. I'll help you get your license."

"My license? What does it matter anyway? I have no intention of ever *practicing* black magic or magic or witchcraft or whatever it is."

"It's not black magic or witchcraft. Those words have negative connotations. We're from an enchanted line of souls who can use energy to heal, restore health, or make a change. And besides, you don't have much choice, Sis."

"What do you mean, I don't have much choice?"

"We need you. There's danger."

"Danger?" Febe felt her heart muscles contract.

"Yeah. There's a lot to go through right now, but... we need the power of seven witches to fight this evil hunter or we'll be eliminated for good, wiped out, like the vampires. So few of them left today."

"Excuse me?"

Wonderful. She just found out that she was part of a family line. But that family line was on the brink of being extinct.

Janvier grabbed her coffee and sat on the couch with her boots still on. "But you must be sworn to secrecy."

"I don't get it."

"You will soon. Now that you've come of age, you're in danger. You're one of the last of the Summer Witch bloodline, Sis. I have a sneaky suspicion that mom's death wasn't accidental, but that's another matter. Come home now."

"What about the apartment? My things? I need to leave the key for my landlord, disconnect the phone line."

Janvier pointed her finger at the phone and uttered something under her breath. She couldn't quite make out what it was. It sounded more like Latin.

"Commanderio finitiora."

A faint light ignited from her sister's fingertip and Febe swore there was a burst of electricity that zinged out of it. An intense energy lingered in the room and seemed to fly onto the counter. The phone jolted.

"Consider yourself disconnected," Janvier grinned.

Febe picked up the phone line only to hear dead silence.

No dial tone. Nothing.

Crap. Her sister *was* a badass witch.

Then...

The room spun. Everything was wrapped up and tied neatly into boxes.

"I'm not supposed to do that," Janvier said.

"Do what?"

"Practice outside of the zone area. But I have no choice. I could lose my license but we don't have much time to pack. You need to leave here tonight. Your life's in danger."

Chapter 8

"My life's in danger?" Febe asked as they exited off the highway toward the small coastal town of Blackshore Bay.

Janvier drove her SUV onto a long country road leading up to the area near the lake dubbed "Cottage Country" because tourists and homeowners would only visit during vacation time. Of course, it was fall so it was quieter. The town of Blackshore Bay was north of Cottage Country. A very quiet, quaint town where most people knew each other.

"Yes, your life is in danger, Sis." Janvier kept her eyes on the road ahead as she drove.

During the trip, Janvier told her sister about their family bloodline and history. Ebony was seated comfortably in the back seat, seemingly watching the trees go by outside as the car sped.

"So Marsha doesn't know yet."

"No. She can't know until she comes of age. By the way, Sis, I'm really sorry about that creepy boyfriend of yours."

Febe sighed. "Don't really want to get into it. He's my past, not my future."

"You know what they say, right? That if he left you high and dry, then he wasn't going to be around for you anyway. Simple as that."

"Not really. I really thought he was the one. He turned out to be a toad instead of a prince when I kissed him. What a loser. Can't believe I didn't see through it." Febe glanced out the window and noticed that they were being followed.

"Oh no."

"What?" Janvier said, casually.

"We're being followed."

"You just realized that?"

"You knew?"

"Yep." Janvier took a quick turn left onto Brock Street.

The black sedan followed them.

Janvier drove further down the road and the black sedan continued to follow them.

They were in trouble. Two young women in the middle of the night on a dark road leading up to cottage country was *not* a good thing. Even if they were witches. Something told Febe there was much worse out there than those who knew magic. She was sure of it.

When they turned onto another road, the car also followed them. Now it was only the girls in Jan's SUV and the sedan on the quiet road. She was certain that as much magic her sister might know, there was nothing that could get them out of that situation alive.

Chapter 9

"You girls lost?" the man came out of his vehicle when Janvier pulled over on the side. He walked up to her window with a flashlight.

The man was tall and had a thick moustache and grey hair. He had a hardened expression on his face.

"Oh, Sergeant Heart," Janvier said.

"Sergeant? Heart?" Febe repeated, quietly.

Janvier glanced at Febe, then turned her attention back to the open window.

"No, sir. We're not lost."

"You do realize there's a curfew up in these parts of the woods."

"Yes, sir."

"Can I see your registration?"

"Sure." Janvier was polite and sweet as pie as she reached into the glove compartment and handed the sergeant the information he requested.

He cast a glance at Febe, narrowing his eyes. He looked at the registration information and back at Janvier. "Don't let me catch you out at this time of the night again."

"Yes, sir. Sorry about that, sir."

When he moved back to his vehicle, he started his car and made a three-point turn and moved away in the opposite direction.

"What was that about?" Febe couldn't wait to ask her sister.

"That's the new sergeant for Blackshore Bay's Police Department. He's a real peach," she said, sarcastically.

"He doesn't live up to his name."

She winced. "There have been a lot of changes in the Bay, Sis. I think you need to know. Tension's been high. There have been a lot of strange things happening and people have blamed it on witches or wannabes practicing black magic.

"Really?"

"Yeah, and it doesn't help that the Gossiping Gosnik family have been spreading their lies and propaganda in their newspapers.

"They're still around?"

Febe remembered the Gosniks. They weren't kind people. They owned a gossip rag of a newspaper and online website that loved to dish the dirt on the town residents. It was almost comical. A show. Unfortunately, people bought into their stories. They used to tell tales about the Summer family, too.

One of the Gosnik sisters had a confrontation with their mother a long time ago at the Summer Café and their mom told them not to come back until they had some manners. Well, since then, they'd tried to spread lies about the Summer Café and their food, saying it was bewitched or something. But that faded with time and they'd moved on to other things...at least Febe hoped so.

Janvier then started her engine again and was on her way, but then she hit something.

"Oh, no."

Janvier stopped the car and got out.

"What is it? An animal?"

The girls moved closely to whatever it was blocking them in the road.

It was a body. A dead woman.

Chapter 10

"Now, you're sure you didn't see anything?" Sergeant Heart asked the girls when he arrived back on the scene. He'd already called for backup and the forensics team would be there soon.

"Nope. Not a thing," Janvier said, wide-eyed.

He gave them a cynical look and scribbled something down on his notepad. His radio was making sounds from the dispatch.

Febe didn't want to look at the body, but she glanced again. There was something odd about it.

In the spotlight from the sheriff's cruiser, she could see the woman had long, tangled blond hair. She was on her side, almost in a recovery position, from what Febe had learned in a first aid CPR course. The woman's hands were bloodied. But what was noticeable was a mark on her right hand. Her wedding band was on her ring finger, but beside it, there was a missing ring or a bloody mark all around her other finger. It was as if someone had yanked her ring off her middle finger, which pointed upward.

"Don't go near there. Forensics will be here soon," the sergeant said in a hard tone. He seemed more bothered that she was near the body than that there *was* a body on the road.

"No, I won't touch anything. But..." Febe tilted her head to the side as if to get a better look. "It looks as if something's missing from her finger."

"Don't go near there."

"I won't," Febe said, disappointed that the sergeant didn't even want to look at the dead woman's middle finger.

Just then, another car pulled up.

A taller man came out of his vehicle, an unmarked police car with emergency lights flashing in the window. The man stood probably over six feet tall – a lot taller than the sergeant. Much younger, too, maybe in his mid-twenties to early thirties, Febe couldn't be quite sure. But what she was sure of was that he had the most striking features she'd ever seen on a man. Strong jawbone with groomed stubble, high cheekbones, dark eyes. He had a distinctive look, as if he could be a cover model for GQ or something. He was handsome, but Febe directed her thoughts away from that observation.

Men were so not on her agenda right now. Or probably ever again.

"What've we got here?" he asked the sergeant.

"Well, Trey, we have a female," he said looking at the ID that he'd found on the body. "Age forty. We need to notify the next of kin."

"Hey, that's Gosnik, isn't it?"

"Come again?" the sergeant said.

"The woman whose family owns that gossip site, right?"

"It is? I'm not into those Internet things."

"They also own a newspaper," the other guy said. "Uncle, you really need to get on top of what's going on now."

Uncle?

"That's his nephew, Detective Trey," Janvier whispered to Febe. "He's hot. But I don't trust any of them."

"Why not?"

"Like I said, they're both new to the town. They've made a whole lot of changes since they came here."

"Whatever happened to the old sheriff? Smith, right?"

"Oh, he was like ninety or something. He retired, remember?"

"Oh, right."

"That's the trouble with small towns like these. People keep their posts forever until they die or can't function anymore."

"Got it."

Febe felt uneasy about that. Given what she'd just been through with her last job, she really didn't like any form of nepotism. Didn't matter which company. Okay, so the Summer Café was run by the women in the Summer family, but that was different, right? It was a family-run private business. But this was the law in Blackshore Bay.

Ebony strutted around the area getting her exercise, oblivious to what was going on. Or was she? Now that Eb could talk, Febe didn't know how to read her feline friend.

But right now, Febe had other problems. She'd just left Toronto to move back to Blackshore Bay and already she'd had more trouble than she could handle.

"Ma'am," the detective said while shining a flashlight on the back of Janvier's SUV. "You mind telling me what these boxes are for?"

Febe glanced inside the vehicle. "Those are my things."

"You're going somewhere?"

"I'm coming back. I...I'm moving back to Blackshore Bay. My sister was just helping me move my things."

He looked at her doubtfully. Trey was handsome, but he looked a bit sneaky when he arched his brow. "Really now? In the middle of the night?"

"Is there a time that is specified for moving one's belongings?"

"Not really. But there is a curfew around this neck of the woods. It's been a dangerous place. You'll need to be careful."

"Oh, I will."

The officer got the girls' information and address.

"The Summer House? *You* ladies live up on the hills?"

"Yes. It's our family home, why?"

The sergeant and the detective exchanged glances. "Just be careful when you're travelling in the woods, ma'am," he reiterated.

"Oh, we will."

Chapter 11

"So you just got back into town and you had to kill someone," Aunt Trixie said, sarcastically, when the girls arrived at the family mansion.

The Summer House was a massive Victorian house on the top of a hill. The police had finished interrogating the sisters and the forensics team had arrived on the scene taping off the area with their bright yellow crime scene tape..

"It was a Gosnik," Janvier told their aunts.

Trixie's eyes opened wide.

"A Gosnik? Which one?"

"Not sure. They didn't say."

"Something's very strange about that death."

"You don't say," Janvier said.

"No seriously, Sis," Febe said. "The fact that the sergeant had Gosnik's ID and purse meant she wasn't robbed. It was intentional and probably premeditated."

Febe loved to solve puzzles. She would often do it in her spare time. Studying human behavior was her specialty, after all. At least that's what it read on her degree.

She wondered why the sheriff didn't want to pursue that angle.

"You made a good point, Febe." At least Aunt Eartha was on her side.

"It's nonsense. Gosnik obviously put up a fight, maybe clawed the guy herself and then he just fled without her purse," Trixie said.

"No, I don't think it was that at all," said Febe.

"What do you know? You're an ad executive."

"I actually have a degree in psychology and behavioral science with a minor in criminology."

"Psych and what?"

"Psychology and behavioral science, remember? I just couldn't find work in that field without furthering my studies, so I ended up in advertising."

"What does that have to do with psychology and criminology, apart from the fact that a lot of advertisers use psychology to lure us into buying their products, then charge us criminally high prices."

"Trixie!" Aunt Eartha said, with her hands on her hips. "Would you please leave our niece alone?"

"Sorry, it's just that since she came of age, so many weird things are happening."

"That's because good things are about to happen. Sometimes it's just the storm before the calm. There are five of us now, strong in our magical energies. Soon Marsha will come on board and we'll just need one more. The dark energies know that."

"Pfff." Aunt Trixie had her arms folded across her chest and her chin up.

Aunt Trixie had always had something against Febe since she was young and caught Trixie taking her mother's makeup. When Febe told her mother, Trixie called her a snitch and said she'd put a hex on her.

Up to this point, she'd thought her aunt was just pulling her leg, but goodness gracious, she was a real witch. They all were. Febe really didn't know when she'd get used to that.

Then on the other hand, if what Janvier said was true about Ebony, Aunt Trixie wasn't all that bad.

"There's a rumor that the Gosniks are witches too, although they hide it," Aunt Trixie said.

"Really?" Febe was stunned.

"If that's the case, it looks as if either she was hit by a random attacker or...or worse. Maybe it was the evil hunter who sensed her and hunted her down."

Aunt Eartha shook her head. "That would not be a good thing. It means that time is running out. We could be next."

"Oh, no."

"Let's not think about that right now. It would take a lot to wipe us all out, if that's the case and this was a witch hunt. We still have until next October. We only need seven witches who are in unity with each other to agree to channel our energies and banish the evil hunter for good."

"Seven witches?" Febe repeated.

"Yes. So far there're three remaining Summer sisters out of the four, your mother would have made four but she...is no longer with us," Aunt Eartha said solemnly. "So, after your sister Marsha comes of age, we'll need one more by the next blue moon."

"Blue moon?" Febe asked.

"Yes. A Full Moon occurs roughly every twenty-nine days. If the Full Moon falls at the very beginning of a month, there is a good chance a Blue Moon will occur at the end of the month. So the next Blue Moon is at the end of October of next year."

"Wow!"

"Yes, wow. It is all based on the lunar phases."

"But why is this important?"

"Energy."

"Energy?"

"Yes. As you know, when the sun sets, the moon rises with the side that faces the earth exposed to sunlight. The Moon has phases because it orbits our wonderful planet, which causes the illuminated side to change. The Moon takes about twenty-seven days to orbit Earth, but the lunar phase cycle, new Moon to new Moon, is around twenty-nine days."

"And that's when we come into renewed energies?"

"Yes."

"But what if we can't find another witch by then?"

They all exchanged glances. "It wouldn't be a good day for any of us."

Chapter 12

"That'll be five dollars and fifteen cents, please," Febe said to the nice, elderly lady at the counter the next day.

She knew she didn't have to come to work, but she just couldn't handle moping around the house. Right now, she felt as if she was doing something constructive. At least it got her mind off her troubles back in the city. She was working at another job, how lucky was that? She was glad that she had her family to be there for her when she needed them more than anything in the world right now.

Of course, that also brought a whole new basket of problems of its own. She always knew there was something odd about her family. Didn't everyone feel that way at some point? But she had no idea just how odd her family was. But still, she loved them.

"Thank you, dear," the customer said.

"You're so welcome."

Just then, she heard music.

"Oh that sounds nice," Febe said, humming as a man playing the guitar outside the café strummed beautifully.

The woman turned around. "Oh, that's Yella."

"Yella?" Febe was stunned.

"Yes, I'm surprised you haven't heard him perform before. He's sweet. He serenades all the customers as they come into the café. Such a nice touch. I do hope he finds a real job someday soon."

Febe glanced out the window. There he was playing away. He was well-dressed, considering he was playing on the sidewalk outside the café. He had shoulder-length sandy blond hair and blue sparkling eyes. He looked very friendly. He had a dimple on his cheek as he smiled and sang.

"He's dreamy."

"Yes, he is. What a nice addition to the atmosphere. Too bad that horrible gossip website trashed his work. We love him, though. He performed for our church meeting once. He's a darling. So polite."

"Aww. That's nice. I hope he gets nice tips. You were saying about his work being trashed?" Febe asked.

"You heard about that nasty gossip columnist stabbed in the night on the roadside?"

The woman surprised Febe. "Um....well, yes, it's horrible, isn't it?"

"Good for her. She was always trashing people in her horrible paper. Not one good work or positive article. Trash. Trash. Trash. Well, she's gone now. One less witch to worry about."

"One less *witch* to worry about?" Febe said, incredulously.

The woman took her order. "Yes. She was a witchy woman. So full of herself. Always putting down others in that ragged column of hers. They should shut the whole newspaper down." The woman left, leaving Febe speechless.

"Well, she was very nice," Febe whispered to Janvier who was right beside her at the other till. The cash registers were a bit quiet now since the rush was over.

"Yeah, you'll meet a lot of different characters in here, Sis. Don't worry about them."

"No, I mean..." Febe looked around. She hinted to Janvier to go back to the office at the back of the kitchen so they could speak privately.

"Oh, right. Hey, Bud, watch the registers for us, won't you?" Janvier called out to one of the other workers.

"Sure thing, boss." He took over while Janvier and Febe logged off their registers.

Moments later, they were in the office at the back of the kitchen. Janvier had grabbed a coffee for each of them.

"So what's up, Sis?" Janvier said casually, sipping her steaming hot coffee.

"What's up? Everything. Don't you think it's odd that everyone here seems so...anti-witch?"

"What do you mean?"

"Well, for instance, that customer who said one less witch to worry about."

"Oh, yeah, that."

"Yeah, that?"

"Oh, Sis, come on now. You need to get used to it. Not too many people around here are fond of witches."

"Yeah, well what about pinning everything negative on witches."

"You'll get used to it."

"What if I don't want to get used to it? I mean I guess it didn't matter before I found out...about my background, but now that I know, I think it's important to set people straight so they don't keep feeding that negative stereotype about all witches being evil and deserving bad things to happen to them."

"Okay, you've got a point, kiddo. But don't get yourself sick trying to correct everyone and please, whatever you do, don't let anyone know about...our background."

"She's right, my dear niece," Aunt Trixie's voice sounded before she waltzed into the back office in her long, flowing fall dress and caped coat.

"Aunt Trixie," Febe said. "What are you doing here now? I thought you had an appointment."

"I do, but I just thought I'd stop by to see how you're getting on in your first day back. You know running a café in the middle of tourist season isn't the easiest thing."

"I didn't know it was tourist season here."

"Oh, come on, child. How long has it been since you've been back? You know it gets busy around here during all the seasons: summer, fall, winter and spring."

"Well, not so much spring," Janvier corrected her auntie. "Definitely summer and fall though."

"Why summer and fall again? Remind me."

"Summer for obvious reasons. Being that it's cottage country season. And the fall because of Halloween. You know with the old monument in the middle of town."

"Oh, that witch burning monument."

"Not exactly. It was during the time of the Salem Witch Trials. Witch burning was so popular back in the day. The town was founded by a witch, as legend states. Anyway, she was burned at the stake, but exonerated posthumously almost a century later. Anyway, many tourists flock to town hoping to catch a glimpse of her spirit."

"Her spirit?"

"Darling, where have you been all these years?"

"Studying in private school in the big city, remember? Then I went straight to university."

"Yes. Right, right. Anyway, as I was saying, many people believe that witches still exist, but because of witch hunters who also still exist, we can't be too careful."

"Witch hunters?"

"People who know we exist but don't want anyone else to know. They try to get rid of us. Lock us up in prison or something for something we didn't do."

"But how do we know who they are?"

"We don't, child. That's why you must be careful."

"But Aunt Trixie, this customer said earlier that she was glad that Darla Gosnik was dead and that she was one less witch to take care of."

Aunt Trixie's skin turned pale. For a moment, Aunt Trixie was speechless. She then walked over to the window and gazed out as if daydreaming.

"Aunt Trixie, are you all right?"

Janvier took a slurp of her coffee and leaned back in the chair in the office. "Nope, she's not okay."

"Why? Did I say something wrong?"

"Not exactly," Aunt Trixie spoke and turned around to face Febe. "You see we've had a rivalry."

"A rivalry? What sort of rivalry?"

"This is what concerns me about her...death. She was in fact a witch."

It was Febe's turn to be gob-smacked. "She was a witch? Are you sure? How do you know this?"

"We figured it out." Janvier took another slurp of her coffee.

"Whoa, wait a minute. Slow down. What do you mean you figured it out?"

Aunt Trixie spread out her fingers and showed Febe her beautiful gold rings. But there was one ring that was the most unusual. It sparkled and had an unusual looking rhinestone embedded in it. "Real witches wear this, child."

"What?" Febe was stunned. She leaned closer to have a look at Aunt Trixie's rings, particularly the funny looking gold ring on her baby finger. She tried to grab it but it wouldn't come off.

Aunt Trixie then removed the ring without effort. "Here, try it on."

Febe took the ring and tried to put it on her finger. It wouldn't go on. It was as if a magnet was pulling the ring away from her skin. Her body tingled, her limbs felt weak and numb and sweat began to pour down her face. "Oh, my God. What is this thing? It's...it's bewitched!" Febe cast it away from her but instead of falling to the ground. It defied gravity and lingered in air for a moment then it magically found its way back on Aunt Trixie's baby finger.

"You see, darling, you're not yet a fully licensed witch. You haven't received the magical blessing officially, so it wouldn't call to you."

"But...but..." Febe glanced at her sister's hands. There were several rings on her fingers but none on her baby fingers. "Janvier doesn't have one. I thought she was a licensed witch now."

"I am." Janvier then pointed to the middle ring finger. "My magical ring is on my middle finger. You see it differs from witch to witch."

Febe felt faint. "Okay, I am so not getting this." She eyed her sister's ring with suspicion. The ring was gold and sparkled just like Aunt Trixie's but was a little different. It had several sparkly rhinestones embedded on it too.

"So anyone who wears a ring like this on any one of their fingers is a witch?"

"No. Not exactly, my dear. You see it depends on which ring is called to you and which finger. Each finger represents a certain vein in your body. The ring finger goes to the heart. That's why it was historically used as the finger of love and where most people wear their wedding ring. Symbolically for the heart."

"Oh, I see. I get it."

"Each of us is unique."

"So, anyone can tell who's a witch then?"

"No."

"No?"

"No. Not so easy, dear. Only witches and warlocks and demons can tell."

"Oh, God. This is getting crazier than I thought. All I did was wake up this morning. Why is this happening to me?" Febe took another sip of her coffee. "So you're saying there are demons now?"

"Oh come now, darling. There are angels in this world who are kind and caring and there are scammy people who are abusive and behave, counterintuitively, against humanity. What do you think is the reason? They are possessed by demonic spirits. But that's another matter altogether. Right now, you need to worry about your courses from the ministry to get your license. We will protect ourselves from these evil souls once and for all so they no longer pose a threat to us. Once we have the seven witches."

"So what about Darla Gosnik?"

"That's a great concern to me," Aunt Trixie said. "You see, I've had many husbands as you know."

"So?"

Aunt Trixie smiled. "I wish everyone thought like you, my dear niece. Anyway, it's bad enough to have to deal with multiple heartbreaks but then to have gossips make it worse by spreading malicious rumors."

"Like what?"

"She basically said that I chased my husbands away because of my cats."

"Yeah, she accused Aunt Trixie of loving her cats more than her men," Janvier added.

"As if that didn't hurt enough. I divorced them all but, well, I found out they were only after my money."

Aunt Trixie had managed to do well in the big city as a hedge fund consultant, but she decided to quit and take her huge nest egg home. She splurged instead on her cats and other pets and the eclectic design of her house next door to the Victorian. Rumor had it that she was one of the wealthiest women in the city, thanks to the newspaper owned by the Gosniks. Then, of course, she married men who seemed as if they were only after her money. Truth was, she didn't have much money now.

"So what if you divorced the gold diggers? That doesn't make you a bad person."

"It does if they disappeared..." Aunt Eartha showed up at the door with a concerned look on her face.

"Hi Aunt Eartha," Febe said.

"Hi, darling. I was looking for your Aunt Trixie. I see you're here troubling the girls."

"I'm just explaining to them about Darla and her vicious rumors."

"So did your ex-husbands disappear?" Febe asked.

Aunt Trixie sighed heavily. "I don't know where they are right now. But I did not kill them as Darla Gosnik implied in one of her vicious gossip columns."

"Oh, no. Aunt Trixie, that makes you look like a..."

"A suspect. I know. I thought about it when I heard that one of them was killed. One of the Gosnik chicks." She ran her fingers through her curly hair. "But I'm not going to worry about that. She has plenty of enemies who would've wanted her dead."

Febe thought back to the scene with Darla on the ground and the missing ring from her finger. Chills ran down her spine. "Aunt Trixie, Darla didn't have any rings on her finger. There was a bloody ring mark. It looked as if it might have been pulled off." Which, as Febe now knew, would have been a difficult task unless the ring came off easily once the witch was dead.

"If Darla was killed because she was a gossiping hag who dug up dirt on the wrong person, then that's one thing," Aunt Trixie said, solemnly.

"But if she was killed because she was a witch..." Aunt Eartha added.

"Then it meant that someone who is not one of us knows our secret and will not stop at killing just Darla."

Chapter 13

Febe tried to calm her pounding heart by taking a few deep breaths. Sipping coffee was counterproductive. The caffeine was a stimulant that would only increase her rapid heartbeat.

"You mean they'd try to come after us, too?" Febe asked.

"Yes."

"But that would mean that someone in the witches' inner circle is a spy. Because only few people know about the power of the rings, right?" Febe said.

The horrible thought began to sink into Febe's mind like quicksand, slow and deadly. What on earth had she gotten herself into? This was her family, though. She just thought that moving away from the toxic work politics of the big city was the best thing for her, only to jump from one drama to another. One that could prove fatal.

"Yes, my dear. But let's not think about that right now," Aunt Eartha said reassuringly.

Aunt Eartha always had a calm way about her, no matter what was going on. It was Aunt Trixie that would show the drama she was experiencing inside. If she was upset or if something was wrong, everyone knew about it.

"It's getting busy out there," Bud said as he came to the back. "I'm gonna need some help at the register."

"No problem. We'll be right there," Janvier said as she got up out of the chair.

"Great. Thanks, boss." Bud wiped his hands on his apron before walking back into the kitchen through the swinging doors to the café.

Janvier finished draining the rest of her coffee then threw the container into the recycle bin and walked out into the kitchen towards the café dining room.

"Are you sure you're all right, dear?" Aunt Eartha asked Febe, tilting her head to the side.

"Yeah, I'm good, Auntie. I'm good, considering the week I've had."

"Your week?"

"Yeah, you know, I've been fired from my wonderful job at the ad agency in the city, lost my wonderful fiancé to my boss, Amanda Miss Perfect Harlington, lost my apartment because I could no longer afford the rent, and now I'm back in my hometown where I haven't been since childhood, only to find out that I'm a wanted witch!" she said with a grin. "Other than that, what's that saying mom used to preach?"

"Count your blessings, not your troubles, my dear. The blessings always outweigh any troubles you might have." Aunt Eartha's grin was even wider. "I'm glad you managed to keep your sense of humor, my dear. You will need that in this world we're living in. It can be dark at times. We need to carry our own light."

"Great. I'll remember that." Febe was genuine in her answer. Sometimes she could get a bit cynical, but Aunt Eartha was right. There was a lot to be grateful for. "I don't have much to complain about because I have family that cares about me. That's more than some people have."

"You sure do, darling niece," Aunt Trixie said. "And don't you ever forget it either. We may not have much but we have each other."

"Now you know that's not true, Trixie dear," Aunt Vanity said as she came into the office. "You have tons of money stashed away in your secret account somewhere."

"Hah. That's not true. I gave most of it away, remember?"

"Oh, right, that silly Save the Cats charity."

"It's a wildlife fund that I set up for cougars."

Aunt Vanity rolled her eyes as she came into the office. "Whatever."

"Hey Aunt Vanity," Febe said, noticing the beautiful, bold golden ring she wore on her index finger with the sparkly design just like Aunt Trixie's, Aunt Eartha's and Janvier's.

Great, now more than ever Febe was aware of her own bare fingers. She had no jewelry, especially the special ring. Not having one on her finger made her different from every member of her family. But she tried to remind herself that she'd earn it one day. She'd get that ring on her own finger soon. That was if she passed her courses. The trouble was, after finishing up a tough degree at uni, she wondered if she had anymore brain power inside her to go further into more studies. She had been looking forward to giving her brain a rest from studying.

"Hey yourself, darling," Aunt Vanity said. "Don't forget we have to bring some sandwiches and refreshments to the *Gosnik News* Headquarters."

"The *Gosnik News*?" Aunt Trixie sounded alarmed. "We're not still going there, are we?"

"You're not, but our darling niece is. And so am I. They ordered lunch to be delivered today for their big meeting."

"But don't you think they would have cancelled it? I mean, given the fact that...that..."

"That Darla Gosnik was found dead?" Aunt Vanity finished for her. "Nope. Just spoke to the news director there. It's business as usual. The show must go on."

"This is great," Febe said, feeling a jolt of enthusiasm. "Maybe we can ask some questions about what stories Darla was working on before she..."

"Oh, no. We will do no such thing," Aunt Vanity snapped. "You're not going to try to investigate this murder, Febe. I know you. Ever since you were a little girl you always had that curiosity gene inside of you, just like your mother. Always had to snoop around and try to solve mysteries. Well, not this one. We're going into the *Gosnik News* office and we're going to deliver their order of Summer Café gourmet sandwiches for their annual meeting and we're going to be nice to the folks there and not question them and leave without any trouble..."

"Oh, I get it," Aunt Trixie interjected. "You just want to flirt with that hot, new editor who works at the newspaper. What's his name? Bruce, right?" Aunt Trixie narrowed her eyes at her sister.

"I do not," Aunt Vanity protested. "I'm not *man crazy* like you, my dear sister."

"Man crazy?" Aunt Trixie shrieked. "How dare you!"

"How dare *you*?" Aunt Vanity leaned toward Aunt Trixie, her hands on her hips and her lips pouted.

"All right now ladies," Aunt Eartha interjected. "Enough now. We have enough to worry about, with attacks against our kind. We don't need to be enemies with each other, tearing each other apart."

"Vanity, you will not be making fun of Trixie's previous relationships and Trixie, you will refrain from making accusations about Vanity. Understood?" Aunt Eartha was in between her sisters, stopping the both of them from tearing each other down.

Aunts Trixie and Vanity had never got along. It used to be her mother who played referee between them. Still, she was glad that Aunt Eartha was there now. What would she have done to stop them from getting at each other if Aunt Eartha wasn't there? They were all witches. She was powerless against them. Okay, she was a witch, too, but she'd only just come of age and had a lot to learn and wasn't even allowed to practice magic yet. She was still buzzed over what her sister did yesterday in packing up her apartment with the twitch of her finger.

Febe sighed. "Fine. We'll just deliver the sandwiches. But I want to speak to the managing editor to at least give our condolences. That was Darla's older sister, Amy, right?"

"Yes, I believe that was her name," Aunt Vanity said, smoothing her hair and straightening her blouse. She couldn't resist glaring at Trixie, though.

Febe rolled her eyes. *Oh, boy. Here we go.*

Febe was glad that Aunt Trixie lived in the house next door to the Victorian and not in the same house as Aunt Vanity and Eartha, or else there would be no peace.

* * *

After Febe washed her hands, she went into the kitchen to help the staff put together gourmet pastrami sandwiches on rye topped with a pickle. They used ultra-smoky, super-seasoned pastrami with fresh lettuce, cucumber, tomato, and a dab of

Dijon mustard. Each sandwich was cut into triangles and placed decoratively on the tray. For dessert, there was a tray of fresh pastries, custard-filled chocolate chip donuts, and a basket of fresh fruits.

"Looks delicious. Makes me hungry," Aunt Vanity said as she got her tray together to take to the car.

"You're telling me."

Just then, the door chime sounded in the café. Febe could hear a deep, authoritative voice in the dining room, but couldn't hear what was being said. All she heard was, "She's in the kitchen," from one of the staffers.

The door swung open and in came a swoon-worthy tall, dark and handsome man in a tailored suit. She caught sight of his badge clipped to his belt.

Crap.

A cop.

Wait a minute. It was dark when they'd been pulled over yesterday, but she remembered now where she had seen tall, dark and handsome before. He was the detective from last night.

"Ms. Summer," he said to Febe.

"Hi there. Detective Trey, right?"

"Yes."

"And I'm Vanity Summer, Febe's young auntie." Aunt Vanity was practically drooling as she extended her hand to shake his, the other hand fixing up her recently permed hairdo.

"Nice to meet you ma'am," he said, shaking her hand.

"Likewise. Ooh, I love a man with *strong* firm hands. *Huge* hands, too," she practically purred.

Febe flushed ten shades of red.

Good God. This is so embarrassing.

Maybe Aunt Trixie was right about Aunt Vanity. Really? Flirting with a detective? Okay, he *was* hot, but still.

Febe cleared her throat. "You're here to ask me some more questions?" she finally asked Detective Troy who tried to get his hand out of Aunt Vanity's strong grasp.

"Um, Aunt Vanity. We should be loading the trays into the delivery car, right?" Febe said.

"Oh, yes, of course," Aunt Vanity said, twirling her hair with her other hand.

She finally let his hand go and eyed him up and down flirtatiously before grabbing a tray of sandwiches and heading out through the swinging doors. Febe was afraid that Aunt Vanity would bump into something on her way out and drop the edible masterpieces they'd just assembled together.

"Sorry about that," Febe said, with a tone of humiliation.

"Hey, no worries. Your auntie has a firm grip."

Yeah, on men, it appears. "I know."

"I'm not actually here to see you, Febe. I'm here to see your aunt Trixie."

"Did someone call my name?" Aunt Trixie said stepping out of the office at the back of the kitchen.

Did the walls have ears? Did Aunt Trixie hear everything that was going on in the kitchen while Febe and Aunt Vanity were preparing the sandwiches?

"Yes, Trixie Summer?"

"Yes," Trixie said cautiously.

"Detective Trey Heart from the Sheriff's office." He showed his badge.

"Hi, sir."

Aunt Eartha also came out, surprised. "Is everything okay here, Officer?"

"I just need to ask a few questions, if you don't mind."

"Sure, please ask away. It's just us girls here. We don't keep any secrets from each other," Aunt Trixie said.

"That's fine. I'd like to know where you were between the hours of ten and midnight last night."

Aunt Trixie's face fell.

Febe watched in horror. She knew she had to leave soon to go help Aunt Vanity deliver the lunch to Gosnik News, but...

"I...I was at my house."

"Do you have anyone who can verify that, ma'am?"

"What are you saying?"

"It's my understanding that you had an argument last week with Darla Gosnik?"

"Well, of course I did. Gosnik and I always have our little spats. We've known each other forever."

"Did you tell her that you would kill her if she mentioned your name in her newspaper?"

"She's not answering any more questions until she speaks to her lawyer," Aunt Eartha interjected, touching Aunt Trixie's arm.

"That's fine, ma'am, but I'm going to need you to come down to the station."

Suddenly the hot detective was turning Febe's blood cold.

The rest was a blur.

Chapter 14

"Trixie's been arrested?" Aunt Vanity said as they drove towards the Gosnik News office down on Main Street.

"I don't know," Febe said, regretfully. "I had to leave, remember? Aunt Eartha went down to the station with her. Do you think it's a good idea delivering these sandwiches now?"

"Oh, nonsense. Besides, I'm going to let you in on a little secret. Nobody down at the station really liked Darla."

"They didn't?"

"She was a bully and a tyrant. The newspaper was left to the Gosnik sisters and Darla bought out the others' shares and turned it into a cheap gossip rag. It used to be a nice community paper back in the day, then Darla decided to go online and change the direction of the content. It got the whole team in a fit. Anyway, she used to dig up dirt for some popular celebrity site down south and decided after her folks passed away that she'd try to build her own little empire."

"Really?"

"Yes, really, child. I wouldn't be surprised if one of them bumped her off. I'm sure they'll welcome us with open arms. She made a lot of enemies out of the other Gosnik family members."

"And what about this new editor?"

Aunt Vanity flushed. "Oh, Bruce. Well, he is really fine. Nice gentleman. We got to talking a little when we catered their company baseball event in the summer. He just joined the paper recently, but he was thinking about leaving too."

"Why?"

"Well, they all were thinking of jumping ship, girl. Weren't you listening? None of them liked the direction the newspaper was going with Darla's vision of turning it into an online gossip site."

"I see."

It bothered Febe that she didn't know what was going on with Aunt Trixie down at the station. She hoped her auntie wasn't under arrest.

"I hope they find out who really killed Darla. I know it wasn't Aunt Trixie. It's possible somebody could be trying to frame her because of that public argument they had. Were you there at the time?"

"Oh, that. Yeah." Aunt Vanity rolled her eyes. "Trust Trixie to always run her mouth a mile a minute.

Anyway, with all her exes vanishing off the face of the earth, maybe the cops are extra suspicious"

"All of them?"

"Yes, all of them."

"Isn't there some sort of investigation into their...being missing?"

"Nope. Nothing suspicious."

"Nothing."

"Not according to the police. They all had homes in the Caribbean. Cops figured they took their share of her money and took off."

"Oh, that is odd."

"Your Aunt Trixie's odd, dear. Get used to it. I don't know where she finds them. She goes travelling on vacation to these exotic destinations. Marries these suckers without knowing their middle name and the next thing you know, they take off back to their homeland, richer than before."

"How do you know that?"

Vanity shrugged, her eyes on the road. "I just do. Well, that's what I read on the Gosnik News site anyway."

"Aunt Vanity!"

"What? Sometimes you get some interesting information online."

"About members of your own family? Really now? You should be ashamed of yourself, reading that stuff and believing crap about your own sister. You yourself said it's a rag site."

Aunt Vanity just shrugged again. Febe knew the sisters weren't the best of friends, but she also knew there was a line they wouldn't cross. Or was there?

Aunt Vanity pulled up at the Gosnik News offices on Main Street.

"I can never park in these spots," Aunt Vanity said.

"What about over there?"

"You expect me to squeeze in there without using magic?"

Febe had to get used to the new way of things now. "Oh, right. Janvier mentioned something about not being allowed to practice magic unless it was an emergency."

"And this is not an emergency, child. Don't ever do anything that could get your license revoked."

"Right. Got it." Febe really had to try to get used to the new normal. If one could call it that.

* * *

"I'm so sorry for your loss," Febe said after they'd laid out the sandwich trays on the table in the boardroom.

Amy Gosnik was a tall, thin woman with jet black hair and porcelain skin with dark makeup. She wore black. She almost looked like a tall, human doll.

"Yes, we're horrified about what happened," Aunt Vanity added, looking around.

"Thank you," Ms. Gosnik said quite enthusiastically. She didn't seem very sad. "Thank you both."

"Do the cops have any leads?" Febe blurted out before remembering that just moments ago her Aunt Trixie was taken in for questioning.

She hoped and prayed that Aunt Trixie would be cleared and the Gosnik family didn't find out about it. But then again, Aunt Trixie had been accompanied by the handsome police detective. It was only a matter of minutes before rumors swirled.

"No, not that I know of," Amy said as she adjusted the sandwich trays on the table at the back of the boardroom with bouncy energy.

"I hope they do find out who did it and fast. What a horrible, terrible thing to have happened," Aunt Vanity added glancing around the room again. "I know this is probably not the best time, but..."

"You're looking for Bruce, right?" Amy said. "He's in his office."

Aunt Vanity self-consciously brushed her coif with her free hand. "Well, we were supposed to speak about placing some ads in the paper for Halloween."

"Yes, of course," Amy said, busily organizing the cups. At each setting there was a glass and a plate along with a file folder and a book. She had the perfect lunch-and-learn set up in place.

"I can help you with that," Febe said, feeling useless.

"No, I prefer to do it myself, thanks," Amy said, hurrying around the table.

Febe noticed that Amy had the utensils and sandwiches pointing toward the east and wondered if that was on purpose. She remembered Janvier telling her once that Amy was a bit OCD when it came to work. They'd worked together before and had gone to the same high school.

After Aunt Vanity left them alone, Amy stopped organizing the table.

Amy then walked over and closed the door of the boardroom. "The meeting will be starting soon, but I wanted to speak with you for a moment."

"Sure. What about?"

"About my sister's murderer."

"Do you have any idea who might have done it?"

"The cops asked me, but I don't know. I read that article and the paper you did for your psych degree on the effects of social media on human behavior. You have excellent research skills. Superior. That's why we, the editors published your findings."

"Oh, no. I don't...I mean I did...well, thank you for selecting the story. That was some years ago."

"Yes. Did you get into the field that you wanted?"

"Well, not exactly." Febe had a sinking feeling in the pit of her stomach. "I do use behavioral research skills in advertising but my dream job would be to...well, it doesn't matter."

"Oh, no. It *does* matter."

"Excuse me?"

"You have a knack for investigative work."

"Not exactly. Behavioral Science *is* the study of human habits, actions, and intentions; and yes it covers the areas of psychology, social work, sociology, and organizational behaviour, but it's not quite the same as police investigative work. I use my skills to study human behaviour when it comes to consumer advertising. Listen, I really think you should speak with the police about this. That much I do know."

"You went into such detail. I'm hoping you can help the cops find the real killer. I have a feeling that..." She looked around nervously. "I have a feeling that there's someone after our family."

"You do?"

"Yes."

Amy finished setting the boardroom table, then led Febe down the hall and into her sister's office.

"I'm surprised it's not cordoned off with yellow caution tape. Did the cops come here to search her office?"

"Yes, but they weren't interested in this." She looked into a file cabinet and pulled out a sheet of paper. She handed it to Febe.

Febe took the sheet of paper and glanced at it. "An article on St. Augustine?"

"Yes."

She read further, "'St. Augustine is a city on the northeast coast of Florida. It lays claim to being the oldest city in the U.S., and is known for its Spanish colonial architecture as well as Atlantic Ocean beaches like sandy St. Augustine Beach and tranquil Crescent Beach.' Nothing unusual there."

"Yes, but she circled the article and placed initials there. HH."

"HH. And you showed this to the cops?"

"We have a new detective and sheriff in town. Now, I'm not saying they're not doing their jobs, but they took the original and said they'd look into it."

"And this is a copy?"

"Yes. The original had the marking in red ink. My sister never circled anything in red unless it was important."

"Hmm. H.H. Oh, wait!"

"What is it?"

What's the sergeant's name again?"

"Will H. Heart."

"Oh, um...nothing." Febe thought it was strange.

"Listen, you have to help us."

"Why do I have to...?"

Amy showed Febe a mark on her skin. "I've just come of age and found out, like you, that I'm...well, magical. My sister just got her ring a while back and now..."

"Oh, God!"

"Yes. That's right. We can't let the authorities know everything about us unless it's pertinent to the case, or they'd lock us all up in jail. Magical folks are still sneered at in this part of the woods."

Febe felt the hairs on her neck stand up.

Chapter 15

"She's magical? Amy Gosnik? Well, isn't that something?" Aunt Trixie said in the living room of the Victorian later that evening.

It was seven o'clock and Febe had an hour to go before retiring for bed. She had to be up for her eight a.m. workshop with Professor Techer. She was told beforehand to get as much sleep as possible for her first session since it would use a lot of intense energy. Whatever that meant.

"Yes, she is. And by the way, Aunt Trixie I am so glad you weren't arrested," Febe blurted out.

"You and me both, sweetie," she said, taking a swig of rum.

"I knew they wouldn't hold you too long," Aunt Vanity said, fixing her coif and glancing into a compact mirror.

Febe swore Vanity must have been bewitched into always checking herself in a mirror. It was unbelievable. No doubt, she must have had a good meeting with Bruce at the paper, because she left there acting like she felt on top of the world. But Febe was smart enough to not ask her how her *meeting* with Bruce went.

"So what did they say?" Febe asked interested.

"It's what *I* said. I had an alibi."

"You mean you stirred one up with witchcraft," Aunt Vanity added.

"Did not."

"Did too."

"How dare you?"

"How dare *you*? You know we're not supposed to use magic for personal gain," Aunt Vanity said.

"And what made you think I did such a thing? You're the one that concocts those ridiculous love potions to try to make men fall for you. I never need such nonsense."

"Ladies!" Aunt Eartha intervened.

Aunt Trixie sucked in a deep breath. "I simply told them I was up late watching TV with my cats and decided to order pizza."

"For the cats?"

"No silly. For *me*. Okay, I might have given them just a little. Well, they actually took a piece off me."

"Aunt Trixie! Garlic is poisonous to cats!"

"I know that, silly. That's why I made sure the pizzas were simple. No garlic in the sauce. It's the meat they like. They usually take off the pepperoni and dig into it. What can I do? I can't deprive them. Anyway, it's fun to watch old episodes of Perry Mason while eating pizza. Nothing like it."

"So what about your alibi?"

"The pizza delivery guy, silly. I just remembered that he came by at that time and saw me there. The Blackshore Bay Pizza remembered my late night call and the guy told his boss about all the cats. I gave him a generous tip, too."

"Good thing, or he might not have remembered." Aunt Vanity made a snarky remark.

"That's not very funny," she shot back at her sister.

"Well, that was a very good thing then."

"Sort of."

"What do you mean sort of?"

"Well, they still want me for further questioning and asked that I don't leave town and to surrender my passport."

"Like witches need passports to fly." Febe grinned. But the joke seemed to be lost on her aunties. Janvier chuckled though.

"Never mind," Febe said dismissively. "I'm glad that you weren't arrested Auntie. I'm really glad about that. I was so nervous when that detective asked you to come down to the station for questioning."

"No worries, dear niece. Your auntie can take very good care of herself."

"And her exes."

"What's that supposed to mean?" Aunt Trixie had her hands on her hips.

"You take care of your exes like Al Capone took care of his enemies."

"Hey, now that's not fair!"

"Ladies, please." Aunt Eartha was getting annoyed now. "Now let's keep things in perspective. The fact remains that someone killed Darla Gosnik and we need to find out who and why. This could be very dangerous if the witch hunters are back in full swing and hunting all modern witches."

"That's true."

Later in the evening, the family had just been treated to a delicious homemade pasta dish by Aunt Eartha with British-styled trifle dessert topped with whipped cream, custard and fresh strawberries with a fluffy cake base. It was scrumptious. Febe felt full for the first time in a while. It was so nice having home-cooked meals for a change and sure beat those cheap packaged noodles on days when she barely had enough to get by on after her student loan payment and rent went through her account. Sometimes she felt like the working poor, just working to exist in the big city on small pay as an intern. But that was all behind her now. She was back home with her peeps in Blackshore Bay.

Ebony, her little four-legged companion was seated cozily by the fireplace in her kitty basket.

Janvier was curled up on the couch, staring into her smartphone like most people these days, waiting for someone to "like" what she just posted on Facebook.

Aunt Vanity was on the far couch, into herself as usual.

Aunt Trixie, who often visited late in the evening before returning to her own dwelling next door, was over by the bar.

Aunt Eartha was seated by the fireplace, too, with a newspaper in her hand.

Febe was seated on the loveseat with her laptop on her lap, scrolling through different search terms on Google. She was eager to get to the bottom of this mystery that could pose a threat to her and her family.

The flat screen TV was on the local news station.

"Our top story today, police still have no suspects in the brutal murder of tabloid queen Darla Gosnik," the reporter announced. "Gosnik was found at the side of the road just outside the town at the border of Blackshore Bay and Main. Police say that she most likely died of asphyxiation. There were obvious signs of trauma..."

"Asphyxiation?"

"Yeah, when your body is deprived of oxygen with can result in unconsciousness and eventually death, often called suffocation," Aunt Vanity said.

"I know what that is Miss Vain." Aunt Trixie rolled her eyes dramatically.

"Hey, that's Vanity to you," Aunt Vanity protested.

"All right you two. I'm trying to listen to the newscast," Aunt Eartha said, her tone laced with annoyance. She was often cool as a cucumber, but Febe felt that she'd probably had enough of her sisters bickering like cats and dogs.

"So someone strangled her?" Janvier said.

"Looks that way," Febe replied. "What strikes me as odd is why was she there late at night?"

"Or was her body moved there?"

"Good question," Febe said, "Unless she was lured there."

"Lured there?"

"Yes. It's not unusual for reporters to meet the sources of their stories late at night."

"But in that neck of the woods? There's a curfew, Sis, remember?"

"I know," Febe said, tapping her pen to her chin. She'd been scribbling down some notes from her Internet searches. "But there was something about the article Amy showed me that makes me think it could have something to do with that?"

"Florida?"

"Yes. St. Augustine, Florida."

"What are you doing?"

"Just looking up some notes about St. Augustine and what could have happened there recently that would make her want to meet a source."

"Okay, you've got to look at it from all angles, niece," Aunt Eartha said.

"What do you mean?"

"It could be anyone who had a motive to want her dead."

"True. She wrote a lot of mean things about a lot of people on her website. I just read a few things. The comments from readers weren't very nice either. Oh wait."

"What is it?" Her aunties eagerly hovered over her computer.

"There was an article written in the last year about Darla's run-in with the law."

"Really now?"

Febe scrolled down the screen. "Looks as if she'd been given a parking ticket at one time and she tried to fight it."

"So?"

"So, she said some unkind things about the parking enforcement officer."

Aunt Eartha leaned in closer. "James Heart, parking enforcement officer. Oh, another Heart family member. Seems like they have their whole family working down at the precinct. I like 'em. They're good folks."

"But look at this comment." Febe scrolled down to a J. Smith from St. Augustine, Florida.

The Hearts are good people. They're all heart, witch is more than I can say for you.

-J. Smith, St. Augustine, FL

"Do you see that? Do you see how that person spelled which?"

"I see. Good catch."

"They used the witch spelling. Ha! That's nothing new. Some people do that to be bitchy or to prove a point."

"But do you think that person knew?"

"Doubt it."

"Another person wrote she should pay her darn tickets and stop complaining. There's a good reason they issue tickets."

"Do you really think that might have something to do with it?" Janvier asked, dubiously. They all hovered on the couch looking over Febe's shoulder at her laptop now.

"To be quite honest, I don't know what to think," Febe admitted. She felt discouraged about the case now. "I don't think that could possibly be related."

"Maybe it's nothing, darling niece. Let's face it. We may never really know what happened to her. It was late at night in a wooded area that had a curfew for a reason. Bears and all kinds of wild animals are known to be in that area."

Febe shook her head. "But she had to have circled the article for a reason – and in red ink. Her sister Amy said she never did that unless it was something important. She regarded newspapers as sacred and would never scribble on them. That's what Amy said."

"Maybe it was Amy who did it." Aunt Vanity moved back to her chair and began filing her nails.

"Why would her sister kill her?"

"Oh, come now. We all know what a wretch Darla was to her sisters. She took over the respectable, family-owned newspaper after their parents died and turned it into some cheap tabloid rag. The police should look into the Gosniks and their alibis." Aunt Vanity continued to file her nails. "I mean the killer would know that she's a witch. Maybe they pulled off her ring because they didn't think she deserved it because of her bullying ways and they wanted to throw the cops off the right trail."

Febe thought about that for a moment. "Amy did seem rather bouncy when we went to deliver the sandwiches for her boardroom meeting. But..."

"But what? There you have it. She's guilty as sin."

"But just because people behave a certain way..."

"Oh there you go with your behavioral science crap..."

"Vanity!" Aunt Eartha called out. "It's not crap. She does have a point. We need to be more supportive."

"Fine. Fine."

Febe felt a headache coming on all of a sudden.

Maybe she really needed to just lie down for a while and not think too much. She had way too much on her brain for this. She'd just lost her apartment, her fiancé and her job this week and now she was back home in her small town and in the middle of a murder. Okay, she didn't do it and she hoped and prayed no one she knew committed it, but she and her sister Janvier were the ones who stumbled on the body. That made it her business. What if that were she? What if they had been the target and Darla just happened to be in the way?

"You know I do think it was pretty strange that the sergeant just happened to be in the area."

"Well, of course, darling. He patrols the area."

"But he was following us."

"And he was probably wondering what two young women in an SUV were doing at that time of night just on the border of the town, driving on that road."

"Okay, you've got a point," Febe said, "I just have some trust issues right now."

"Ha! I knew it. That guy really did a number on your heart, didn't he? Well, just because you met one slimy guy, doesn't mean they're all like that. Most men, especially small town men, are pretty nice," Aunt Vanity said.

"You should know," Aunt Trixie snuck in her comment.

"And what's that supposed to mean?" Aunt Vanity placed her hands on her hips, furiously.

"Never mind."

"Fine, then keep that pucker of yours shut."

"Excuse me!"

"You heard me."

"Ladies, please!" Aunt Eartha called out again.

Just then Aunt Trixie got up and swiftly moved, her long cloak swinging and hitting the glass on the coffee table.

The glass was about to fall on Ebony.

Febe panicked, her eyes widened. A strange energy zoomed through her and the cup froze in midair.

The ladies in the room all had their eyes wide open and their jaws on the floor.

What. Just. Happened?

Chapter 16

The next morning, Febe woke up feeling more tired than she'd ever felt before. Of all the inventions and magic in the world, they still couldn't invent something that could make people just bounce right up out of bed with enough energy, caffeine-free. She'd hit the snooze button one too many times. It was time to get up now.

She yawned and stretched after she pulled the covers from her and swung her feet over the side of the bed.

Her mind was still reeling from what had happened last night.

Did she cause the glass to freeze in midair? Did she *really* do that?

It totally freaked her out.

Her aunties had explained that she was quite advanced for someone who wasn't yet fully licensed. They told her that her skills and drive to protect those close to her was superior. Not all witches had the same strengths and gifts.

She certainly did have a gift. That made up for all the crappy feelings she'd had this week.

Was that what happened when her now ex-fiancé tried to pull one over her at his condo after she'd walked out of his apartment? Did the door slam in his face because he was about to do more harm to her? Either emotionally *or* physically?

She yawned again and placed her feet into her slippers at the bedside. She saw Ebony move a bit at the foot of the bed. Sometimes she slept in her kitty bed, but last night she crept up on Febe's bed. Probably just grateful to have not had a glass smashed into her last night.

Ebony yawned and told her, "Good luck with your class today!"

"What?" Oh, right her cat could talk. She had to get used to that.

"I can talk, remember? Stop looking so surprised every time I open my mouth and talk like a human. At least I've always got useful things to say."

Febe blinked once emphatically. Ebony was talking a bit more now.

"You need to get used to it, girl," Ebony said. "And by the way, I owe you big time. Huge thanks for saving my head last night. Though I've got nine lives, don't want to use them all up, you know."

"Um. Right. Uh...you're welcome."

"Oh, and eat well. I've been *dying* to tell you that before I could really talk to you, but better late than never. That crazy junk you ate, packed with caffeine and sugar. No wonder you were always strung out on fatigue," Ebony said, her tone tinged with a purr.

Okay. My cat's bitching at me. Like is this for real? My cat's bitching at me.

Deep breath, Febe. Deep breath.

"Bet you were hoping when you woke up this morning, it would have all been a dream. You would be back at that unappreciative day job with a bitchy boss and sleazy fiancé and low pay and everything in your apartment you can't even afford and a cat that doesn't talk back to you, huh?"

"Um. Yeah. You could um...say that."

"You are what you eat. Remember that? God, it ticked me off watching you eat crap and expecting to feel like jewelry. You want to look good and feel good, you have to eat good."

"Okay, okay. Got it."

"Don't think you do, Sis. Abs aren't made in the gym. They're made in the kitchen."

She rolled her eyes. "I suppose you'll be following me to the kitchen then?"

"You got it. Madam Techer or Professor Techer is a real stickler for punctuality and preparedness. Better eat well and save your energy because you're gonna need it."

"Oh, boy. Will I ever."

"You'll do just fine. Besides, it's not your typical classroom. It's a cozy Victorian like this one. Class size is small. Usually one student at a time."

"Oh, well, that's...different."

"Yeah, don't sweat it."

"I won't. I'll try not to."

* * *

Febe made her way down the corridor to the bathroom. She glanced at herself in the mirror; her ebony hair was all over the place now. She wished she had a magic wand to just tap it to make it look combed.

She grabbed her red toothbrush and scrubbed her teeth in proper motion, thinking about her newfound abilities now. What did this really mean? Was it possible to get her morning routine done without lifting a finger? Nah! That would be silly. Pointless.

She remembered what her sister told her about using magical gifts wisely. Not being able to practice without a good purpose.

That's it. Practice with Purpose. She would have to remember that. The last thing she would want to do was to get her license revoked before she even got it.

Imagine that! Having a license, a right to practice *magic*!

It was surreal. Unbelievable. She finished brushing her teeth.

She was a witch now.

She wasn't the same woman she was the week before. She had to get used to it. Though she felt the same. Except, of course, during the times when she would get intense headaches and then feel this weird zing of energy course through her blood with lightning speed. That was something she didn't think she could ever really get used to. And just to think that was just the tip of the iceberg. There was more to her life than just that. Sheesh.

After she finished her shower, she got out of the bathroom and toweled her hair and her skin. She felt a cool draft blow into the bathroom.

She glanced at the window, which was closed when she first came into the bathroom this morning. But now...

It was opened.

She walked over to the opaque window and closed it.

"That's weird."

She didn't think much of it at the time but would ask her aunties later if any of them opened the window in the morning. She knew Aunt Vanity loved to have hot, steamy showers. Maybe she opened the window earlier and Febe didn't realize it was partially opened, then the October breeze probably blew it wide open. Still, she was on the first floor of the house. It creeped her out a bit.

Right now, her aunties were at the Summer Café tending to customers. They often left early to ensure everything ran smoothly in the morning rush. They had employees open up the café at five a.m., but they liked to get there early, too. When her mother founded the café, she wanted it to be a family business run by the family in a family-friendly environment. Her sisters wanted to keep it that way.

Febe missed her mother like crazy. It had been so long since her mother died now. But she tried not to think about that right now. Ebony just told her to keep her energies topped up and truth be told, she always felt a damper on her energy when thinking about losing her mother.

* * *

After a quick breakfast, Febe left the house and made her way up Chancery Lane toward a house on the hill. Ebony told her it was a cozy Victorian home just like the one they lived in now.

Well this one was an old red-brick Victorian-era house like the one her family lived in, but this one was different. Way different.

It looked a little creepy, to be honest. She didn't know what it was, but something about it was weird.

The house stood on its own on top of a hill overlooking the bay. It was surrounded by white picket fences all around and had green-painted shutters on all the windows.

She thought she saw someone look out of the top attic window. A woman in a white gown stood at the window staring at Febe as she walked up the pathway. Was that Madam Techer?

As she neared the house, the front door swung open. Another woman stood in the doorway, she had a jovial smile on her face and her arms folded across her chest.

"You must be Febe Summer. I've been expecting you." The woman's voice was warm and friendly. Her cheeks were rosy red.

She resembled Meryl Streep. Her hair was shiny and blond with some silver streaked in. Her lipstick was red as strawberries. Her eyes were blue as the ocean.

"Hi," Febe said. She took off her backpack. She didn't know what to bring, so she just took out her old university backpack with her ring binders. She was told beforehand there would be a lot to take note of.

"Oh, you won't be needing anything in your backpack," Professor Techer said as Febe walked into the foyer.

Their shoes clunked on the shiny, pine-scented hardwood floor. She noticed the fine, outdated velvet drapes at the window. The inside had an antique, Victorian feel to it.

Madam Techer wore a long black dress, buttoned up to her neck. Her hair was done in an upsweep.

"I won't?"

"Oh, no. You have the best note taking software and tools up here," she said, pointing to Febe's mind. "Your mind is the greatest computer ever created and can store up to three trillion facts, autocorrect errors that you see, visualize and create things. It can store countless memories and change your reality just by thinking. Your brain is thirty times more powerful than the best super computer out there. We only use ten percent of our brains. Some...less than that."

Febe grinned.

"Thoughts are potent, my dear. Some things are better left stored in the mind. You don't want to leave traces of our lesson on paper for others to see." She arched a brow.

"Right. Of course," Febe said, feeling sheepish.

"Not to worry." Madam Techer took Febe's bag and placed it on the counter. "I can feel your energy right now, dear. You have a lot of emotional baggage on your brain. It's weighing you down without you even realizing it. You need to master your mind. Your thoughts."

"Now that's a challenge."

"The greatest battle we fight is in our own minds. It's not what happens to us, but our thoughts about it that causes us distress. Think about it. Most babies don't worry or fret about things. They haven't developed thought processes yet."

Febe grinned. "Now that's true."

Febe thought it was odd that there was no sign on the outside or inside that would indicate it was a school of any kind. Or that she held classes there.

Madam Techer then turned around and called out to someone. "Gerard."

An older gentleman, hair greased back and dressed in a black butler's tuxedo, white shirt and bow tie, approached. Febe noticed his shoes were shiny and spotless. "Gerard, will you please fetch us some tea with biscuits and take Febe's bag to the coat room."

"Yes, ma'am."

"Oh, I'm good, thanks. I just had breakfast." She took Ebony's advice and fixed a healthy breakfast with cereal and milk, fruits and nuts and a glass of freshly squeezed orange juice. Unlike her usual city donut and coffee she used to inhale on her way to the subway.

Life in the small town was a nice change of pace. Instead of honking and traffic sounds, she was greeted to the sound of the birds chirping in the distance, the tree leaves rustling in the wind and the sound of the water lapping against the shoreline.

Nature. Calm. Beautiful.

"Um, Madam Techer. There was a woman upstairs in the attic. She was staring out of the window."

"Oh, my sister."

"Your sister?"

"Yes. Why?"

"Oh, um. You keep your sister in the attic?" Febe tried to sound as nonchalant as possible.

This woman was recommended by the Council of Witches. She must be legit.

"Oh, no. She chooses to stay up there. She doesn't like to mingle with folks."

"I see."

Madam Techer led Febe into a massive study with rows of wooden bookshelves lining the walls. There was a large stone fireplace in the center with a fire burning. Above the fireplace was a scenic painting of a palm tree, beach and white house. On the painting was the inscription: St. Augustine. Was that St. Augustine, Florida?

Febe immediately thought of poor Darla Gosnik. She might have been a gossip and a tabloid menace, but no one deserved to be murdered, especially not like that with their body tossed on the side of the road in the middle of the night. Febe took her attention away from the painting. Probably just a coincidence.

"I see something is troubling your mind, dear." She sipped tea from an antique teacup with intricate designs.

"Oh, yes. I guess you could say that."

"Tell me what it is, dear. You need to clear your mind before you begin your first lesson."

"Well, let me see. I found my ex-fiancé cheating on me with my boss. I got fired by said boss. Could no longer afford my apartment in the city and oh, yeah, my family called me to come back here and informed me that I'm really a witch."

Madam Techer placed her cup down and grinned. "You've had a dreadful week, dear."

"Yeah, you're probably thinking I'm a real loser, right?"

"Oh, no. Quite the contrary. I think you're a winner."

"A winner?"

"You're still standing, aren't you? Someone once said that tough times never last, but tough people do, Febe. We all go through hard knocks. That's nothing new. It's those who can still move forward and don't let it sink them who are true winners in the game of life."

"The game of life?"

"Well, there's more to it than just that, of course."

Madam Techer lit a candle in the middle of the room. She drew in a deep breath and appeared visibly uncomfortable.

"Is everything all right, Madam Techer?" Febe said leaning forward.

"I...I always get this way around candles. Fires."

"You do?"

"You sound surprised, Febe. We all have fears, my dear."

"But I thought you said fear is not good?"

"Being courageous and having fear are two different things, Febe. Anyone can have fear, but making a move despite your fear makes you a conqueror."

"That's true, I guess," Febe said, nodding her head.

Madam Techer drew in another deep breath and lit the candle in the middle of the coffee table. She then stretched out her right hand to the bookshelf to her left. "*Commanderio es Shamon.*"

A book wiggled on its spine, then moved itself slowly off the dusty book shelf and floated in midair over to where Madam Techer and Febe were sitting to lay itself on the coffee table.

Febe's jaw fell open in wonder.

She was seeing this, but it was difficult to believe it.

The book then opened itself on the table and the pages started to flip as if an invisible person was turning them until it got to the center of the book. Then it rested there.

Madam Techer had a nonchalant expression, while Febe was still in awe. Complete fascination of what was going on around her. This was her world now, wasn't it? Magic.

She had to get used to it. When *was* she ever going to get used to it?

"Now, you will be doing a seven-part intensive examination to obtain your witching license. So please pay attention. I'll be giving you a crash course so that you have all the necessary knowledge and practice to master your exam. After that, it will be up to you to continue to learn. Learning never stops once you receive your papers, just like when you graduating high school or university. The learning begins in the real world when you apply all that you've learned."

"Right. Got it." Febe tried to focus so that she wouldn't miss anything. The last thing she wanted to do was to goof up on her witching license. Even her Aunt Trixie got her license. Never mind that: Aunt Vanity who was always preoccupied with a mirror had her witching license, too. Which meant, if they could get one, so could she.

"You look worried, dear."

"I am. I just don't want to screw up. My family would never forgive me."

"Nor would you forgive yourself."

"I know. I usually record my lectures at school."

"Like I said before, dear, your mind is the greatest computer and records everything in your subconscious whether you're aware of it or not."

"I guess you could say that."

"Now if there's one thing you need to remember, it is this. Energy."

"Energy?"

"Yes, energy, dear. The world is energy. Our thoughts and feeling, our emotions. That's why whenever you're around negative people, they can drain your energy. Your soul."

"You're telling me. My boss, Amanda, was a real..."

Madam Techer frowned.

"Never mind."

"Good. Now, there are things in this world we can't see, but we can feel them, their effects are everywhere. Once you understand energy, you can use it to your benefit and avoid unnecessary pain."

"How?"

"Firstly, there are two types of energy you need to be aware of. Stored energy and working energy."

"Hey, wait a minute. I dealt with this before in Physics 101."

Madam Techer shook her head. "No no, dear. This is quite different. The stored energy and working energy is more than just potential energy and kinetic energy," she said, obviously a physics master herself. "This is about magical energy. Most people have regular energy to work and go about their daily activities. What sets witches apart is the fact that we have an unusual amount of energy that can turn the mundane into magic. And move objects and make things happen."

"Interesting."

"You will learn this in time, dear." Madam Techer took another sip of her tea and placed her cup down, while the magical book flipped through to another page.

"In the dictionary, energy is defined as the strength and vitality required to sustain physical and mental activity. Changes in your levels of vitamins can affect your energy and well-being so you must be careful."

"I'll try."

"No. Don't try. Do."

"Do?"

"Yes. Just do it. Magic is the art and practice of moving energies to effect needed or wanted change. Remember that."

Febe tried to soak it all in. "Does that include...um...levitation."

Okay, Febe always read about that. She thought it would be so cool to just levitate. Imagine getting through rush hour traffic by just floating above it and swiftly moving to where you had to go. She figured that was probably why witches were on broomsticks. Though it was probably more a metaphor than an actual thing. She'd never seen anyone on a broomstick moving through the skies before.

She grinned. "Yes, we'll get to the power of levitation but that is quite advanced. The key to magic is the ability to raise, manipulate and direct energy."

Febe though about the glass on the table and how she was able to freeze it in midair. Sweet. So she had a bit in her already.

"I see you've done this before by protecting your cat."

"Yes, how did you...?"

She grinned and took another sip of her tea. "Before we can properly cast a spell to make things happen at will, not by chance, we must first learn how to raise our bioelectricity."

"Our bioelectricity?"

"Yes, dear."

"There's a lot to learn."

"There is?"

"There are many different types of energy, but emotional energy is the most powerful."

"Emotional energy?"

"Yes, like the one you used by chance when your ex-fiancé turned on you."

"Oh, right."

"And the one you used by chance because you had to save your beloved cat from an unfortunate accident."

Febe's eyes opened wider.

"Yes, love is the most powerful emotion and can work amazing magic. One can raise their emotional energy by meditating and practicing the art of focus. Allowing yourself to focus on what is good and useful to you, not on negative mindless things that can drain whatever reserve you have for no gain. You'll need that for spell casting."

"Spell casting?"

"Yes, spell casting. We'll also go over pushing energy."

"Pushing energy?" Febe tried to keep track of things in her mind.

"Yes. The ability to move energy using your body with practice. And visualization. I see your power of visualization is already good."

Febe grinned. "I work in advertising, designing ad campaigns."

"Yes, I know. You still have a lot to learn about directing your mind's focus and using your palm to mentally push out force to make things move and happen. But you will need to learn how to replenish your energies."

"What do you mean?"

"What happened after you slammed the door on your cheating fiancé?"

"Come to think of it, I felt drained like a..."

"Precisely. I'm not surprised, dear. You expelled energy without replenishing your stock. Recharging. You need to recharge. You experience a warm, tingling sensation in your hand like pins and needles when you first expel this energy, then...you feel drained like all the power has drained from you."

"Hey, that's exactly how I felt."

"I'm not surprised, dear. One day you will learn to command these energies and call upon them quickly and efficiently to heal and mold before directing it to an intended target or goal. That is the difference in being an established witch, being able to call the powers to use. That is essential for a properly trained witch. One day, you'll become stronger if you don't let yourself down. You'll be able to move energies from your primary hand and both hands. You will learn more control."

"This is just like the night I was supposed to move, when my sister cleaned up my whole apartment in seconds."

Wow, all this time she thought of her sister as just...annoying, into herself Janvier, but the way she commanded her apartment to be cleaned up in seconds like a whirlwind of magic around her was...wow, amazing! She had to give it to her sis: she had renewed respect for her now.

"I'm not surprised."

Febe almost regretted saying that now, hoping that Janvier would not be in any trouble, but then again, she needed to get out of there fast.

"I'm going to give you the opportunity to use the command word *commanderio* for a simple action."

"*Commanderio*?"

"Yes. *Commanderio*. I whispered it to call to my spell instruction book to come off the bookshelf. It allows the energy forces to cooperate with your energy. Now call to your backpack."

Febe swallowed hard. "How am I...supposed...?" She didn't want to mess up her first lesson, but this was hardly a lesson now was it? She was diving into the deep end to see if she could sink or swim. Anxiety got the best of her. Her stomach knotted into twists. She could feel her head spinning.

"Um...commander..."

"No, dear. *Commanderio*. Now say it like you mean it. Feel the energy of your backpack. Command it to come to you. Stand up now."

Both Madam Techer and Febe stood up in the study and glanced at the open French doors.

Febe cleared her throat. "*Commanderio* enter beside me." Febe felt moisture pool on her forehead.

Then suddenly, her backpack slowly shifted itself into the room.

Her eyes widened in shock. Her heart exploded into rapid heartbeats. Did she do that? Was she commanding her backpack to come to her? Or was Madam Techer helping her out?

Then...

The bag stayed put.

"*Commanderio* enter beside me. Now."

Nothing.

Madam Techer had her arms folded across her chest, her chin tilted upward as she glanced at Febe with a slight grin on her lips.

"*Commanderio*."

"Think, dear. Use your emotions. Your good emotions."

How on earth did she get that door to slam between her and Jonathan the other day? Suddenly, the emotions of upset over his betrayal came flooding back but she tried to shift it out of her mind to focus on her lesson.

"*Commanderi*..."

Just then the backpack leaped off the floor in full force and came flying at full speed directly toward Febe.

She tried to duck, but it was too late. It slammed her right square in the face.

"Ouch!" she said as she flew backward, touching her nose with her hand. "That hurt!"

"Yes, the truth can hurt, dear. You must conquer your fears, Febe. You were focusing on the wrong energies just now. The world treats you how you treat it. Everything has energy, believe it or not."

"Everything?"

"Yes, dear. And fear and constant worrying is not the witching way and can drain your energies too. So just be aware of that."

"*Commanderio back*!" Madam Techer clapped her hand and spoke quickly. The backpack lifted off the floor and went back out through the room and disappeared toward where the butler had placed it. Febe could no longer see it.

She got up off the floor, still grabbing her nose. Well, she knew that it would be a pain to go back to school again, she just didn't think it would be literally.

"You need to clear your mind from worry, doubt, and fear if you want to succeed as a witch, dear."

Well that really sucked. She was always worrying about something. Paying her bills on time, making a good impression at work, fitting in. No wonder she wasn't all she could be.

"Some people, like emotional vampires and demonic souls, take energies from others to remain powerful. Good people like witches who heal and help others, take it from the sun, their own internal stores, and the energy of the earth without doing any harm to the source. But we'll also discuss something else that's on your mind, dear. The murder of a woman that crossed your path on your way back to town."

"What?" Febe swallowed. "You heard about that?"

"Everyone has, dear. It's all over town now. News like that is not kept secret. Mind you, her death was not natural."

"You're telling me. She was strangled."

"Oh, no dear. I meant it's not a natural person. Strangulation or asphyxiation might be the police procedural term or the medical term, but we know better. She was killed by a demonic force. One that could easily wipe any one of us out."

Febe's hairs stood up on her neck again. "What do you mean...how did you...?"

"I feel fear around you and feel a negative energy trying to get to you, but you're strong, Febe. You need to keep yourself together. You're a lot stronger than you realize."

"I am?"

"Yes. You have magic blood. Why does that surprise you, dear? Be more confident in yourself."

Febe felt silly for a moment. Was it that obvious that she was self-conscious? She should be like her sister Janvier, self-confident, or maybe like her Aunt Vanity, just full of herself. But oh, no. She had to be the bashful Summer sister.

"You have a natural inclination to want to help others. That is the first rule of witching. A true witch uses her power to heal, help and do no harm. Remember that."

Febe nodded thoughtfully. "But wouldn't that make me an outcast?"

Madam Techer grinned. "Quite the contrary, dear. You see many witches use their gifts in different ways. There are psychics. Some good and some who have misbehaved so they've lost their license to practice and have been cursed in the process."

"Oh."

"And some go into performance but that is frowned upon."

"Performance?"

"Yes. Magic shows and what have you. Some use their gifts to do readings and set up shop, join the circus or showbiz where they won't stand out so much. Some go into the arts and sciences. Some teach. Some go into medicine to heal patients and provide unbelievable comfort. Some go into medical research to help find a cure, but be careful of medical research."

"Why?"

"We once had a witch who tested a drug to help cure herpes. Let's just say it didn't end well. It wasn't a pretty sight. Neither was she at the end of that experiment."

"Oh." Febe gulped.

"Some of us are even hired by the FBI and other law enforcement agencies to work on cold cases," she continued. "They help find victims' missing remains while working with the forces on the other side: the wandering spirits of the victims who direct them to the site of their bodies."

"Wow!"

This all seemed so overwhelming to Febe. But at least she knew she could use her abilities, her gifts to help others. That was reassuring. So much for that dreadful stereotype about witches flying on broomsticks, cackling at the moon with their ugly wart noses and tall black hats. The more she thought about it, the more she realized her aunties were right. They needed to help eliminate those harmful stereotypes and negative media portrayals of their kind. But one baby step at a time. If she ever went back to advertising maybe she could start by changing the way they were portrayed in Halloween corporate ads. Now *that* would be something.

"Just remember that your gifts can have unlimited use with normals."

"Normals?" This was a lot to take in. Nothing about their conversation or about this lesson was normal. But Febe had to get used to this new way of talking now. She wasn't just a girl from the city originally from a small town in Southern Ontario. She was a gifted witch. As crazy as that sounded.

"Yes, normals," Madam Techer clarified. "Witches are known as magical folks and other human beings who did not possess or know how to harness their energies in a gifted way are known as normals or non-magical folks. And just an FYI, it is very hard for the two to mix, in terms of mixed relationships. The Council of Witches doesn't encourage it as it can lead to unfortunate consequences."

Wait a minute. Was she saying that interrelationships between witches and normal folks were prohibited? Well, that threw the idea of ever dating in the future out the window.

"Why's that?" Febe asked.

"We'll get into that at a later lesson, but for now, just think about what you wish to do with your gifts in the future."

"I hope I can help the police solve the case of that columnist Darla Gosnik. I mean, seeing her body like that on the ground..."

"Yes, it was quite unfortunate what happened to her. She wasn't very well liked."

"I gather. She wrote some pretty strong words about a lot of people on her site."

"She was one of us, but had her license revoked."

"She did?" No one told Febe that before. Did her aunties know this?

"You seem surprised."

"I am. Why was her license revoked?"

"Oh, it was a long time ago," Madam Techer said. "She broke rules number twelve and thirteen of the thirteen principles of witching."

"The thirteen principles of witching?"

"Yes, dear. Rules or principles. The term is often used interchangeably. We will go through those in the coming weeks."

"Right. I'll make a mental note of that."

A smile of approval touched her lips.

"Out of curiosity, what are rules number twelve and thirteen?"

"Number twelve is to practice within the magical guidelines. There is power in words and one must use words wisely to bring goodness not evil to others. Number thirteen is self-love."

"She broke those rules? How?" Febe was curious as to how this might have contributed to her murder. Perhaps there was a clue in there somehow, as farfetched as it sounded right now.

"If you have self-love, it is difficult to hate others. Love is something you can't give if you don't have it to begin with. It is not a vain type of love, either. It is a respectful love and the type that makes you want to treat others how you wish to be treated."

"I see. I guess having a gossip column that dug up scandals about others wasn't exactly kosher then?"

Madam Techer took a sip of her tea. "It's unbecoming of a witch and counterproductive to the rule of do no harm."

"One of the principles is to do no harm?"

"Exactly. Her fault was that she went too far, believing that she was helping by exposing other's secrets, faults and weaknesses when in fact she was scandalizing them."

"I take it you weren't a fan of hers at all."

"I'm not going to lie to you, Febe. She hasn't been very kind to my family either. She has written a few nasty articles about the Council, too and about my teaching practice, but witches don't hold grudges."

"They don't?"

"And why does that surprise you? Please don't tell me that you buy into the stereotypes of witches who are evil creatures."

"Oh, no." Febe bit down on her lower lip. "Not really. I mean..."

"It's all right, dear. That's not the only thing that is bothering you, is it?"

"No. I get the feeling that it was no accident that we stumbled on her body the other night when we came into Blackshore Bay. This terrifies me. I mean, was she killed because she was a witch or because of her scandal site?"

"Your aunts have probably already informed you that you need to be very careful. I think you should take that advice seriously."

Febe swallowed hard.

"You see she was not killed because she was a witch. At least I don't think she was initially."

"You mean whoever killed her found out later?"

Madam Techer nodded. "I believe so. Part of the rules of witching is to master yourself, Febe. Perhaps that's an area where you can accomplish more. You have a burning desire to use your abilities and normal gifts to solve problems, just as you did in bringing messages to your client's customers in the advertising business."

"Yeah, only this is murder."

Febe looked up at Madam Techer, whose face was stone cold.

"Madam Techer, are you all right?"

The book on the table snapped shut. "This lesson is now over for this week. You will read over the first few chapters of the *Witches Guide to Magical Spells* by Inerva Hagspeed.

"Excuse me? Is that a book I can actually get from the library?"

"No, no, dear." She sighed deeply. You will go the Ministry website and follow the link. Yes, we do use the Internet like everybody else these days.

Febe grinned. "I sense something's wrong."

"It is. We have company on the curb. I will be off now." Madam Techer got up and gestured to Febe to leave.

"Um...Okay."

When Febe glanced out the window, she saw below at the bottom of the hill leaning up against his police car, the handsome detective from the other night.

Oh, crap! Did he follow her there?

Chapter 17

"Detective Trey, right?" Febe said, walking down the steps from the house with her backpack slung over her shoulder toward the curb where Detective Trey Heart leaned casually against his car.

"Yes, Ms. Summer, we need to stop meeting like this." He gave her a cocky grin.

He looked so gorgeous with his tall muscular physique and chiseled cheekbones, beautiful eyes framed by long lashes. Why was it that guys always had the long, beautiful lashes?

"Yes, we must stop meeting like this," Febe agreed.

Febe could feel the pitter-patter of her heartbeat but tried to ignore her body's response to this Greek god like cop. Why on earth was she having this sort of reaction to him? She wished she could control her body's responses like a spell. But chemistry was always tricky to control. Magic or no magic.

He was still a man and she needed to take a break from men right now. Especially after what Jonathan did to her. She would never be the same again.

Oh, wait. As Madam Techer said, tough times don't last but tough people do. She'd get over that douche bag, but she still was taking a break from men.

Had the detective been following her? Did he suspect her of anything since she found the body with her sister? But then why wouldn't he just come out and say it?

"Mind telling me what you're doing here?" He gestured his chin to the house on the hill.

"Doing where?"

"Up there on the hill."

Febe froze.

She couldn't just tell him that she was taking magic lessons from a witch so that she, too, could get her witch license.

Think Febe, think. Don't lie. But don't blurt the truth, either.
You have the right to remain silent. Silent. Silent.

"I was just visiting someone. Is that illegal?"

He looked around her toward the house with an odd expression as if to say she was crazy. He then glanced back at her.

"You were doing what?" he said slowly and cautiously.

"I...um...was visiting someone."

"Up there?"

"Yes. Up there. In the house."

"What house?"

Febe turned around incredulously. "*That* house on top of the hill."

He chuckled and shook his head. "Ma'am, I'm going to ask you nicely not to go up there again. It's way too dangerous."

"Too dangerous. Why?" Her heart exploded into rapid beats in her chest. Something bad was coming, she just felt it in her bones. "Why?" she asked again slowly, narrowing her eyes suspiciously.

"Because since the house burnt down a century ago, it's not really safe grounds."

"Excuse me?"

"The Techer Sisters owned that place back in the early 1920s until it was burnt down to the ground with them and their butler in it."

Febe's body tensed.

Chapter 18

"So when were you going to tell me that Madam Techer was a *ghost*?" Febe demanded, her hands placed on her hips, an hour later after she left the Techer House on the hill and returned to the Summer Café. She hadn't been able to wait to get her aunties into the office to confront them.

Aunt Eartha looked nervously to Vanity and then to Trixie. "I know we should have warned her ahead of time."

"What on earth for?" Aunt Trixie said. "Then she wouldn't have passed her first test. Her power of imagination is superior. We suggested she would see a teacher who lived in a cozy Victorian and that was what she *saw*. The old house as it stood before it burned down was real to her in her mind—in her reality."

"But it isn't magic, is it? In life people see what they want to see."

"But many can't see what's not there. The Techer house was a burnt down skeleton of the original home filled with rubble and blackened furniture. It was never refurbished. But our dear Febe saw it as it was back in its heyday. Good on you, dear."

"Okay, this is way too creepy for me. I am so not going back there."

"Oh, but you have to, dear."

"No, I don't."

"Yes you do."

When Detective Trey had informed her what the house was. She had slowly turned around and looked at it again. Only it wasn't the nice-looking Victorian House with the red brick exterior and green window shutters. It was an abandoned piece of property with blackened bricks, decaying exterior, boarded up windows, black shutters and a peeling roof. It looked like an abandoned ghost house.

Holy crap. Why hadn't she seen it before?

When she had taken a closer look, she had seen no white picket fence around the property, only boarded up wood with massive cobwebs.

The attic window where she saw Madam Techer's sister – her sister's ghost – staring out, was empty. There was no multi-paned glass there. You could see right through it to a dark inside and another window on the other side.

Thinking about that gave Febe chills right up and down her spine. *Yikes.*

What was wrong with her?

She was seeing things that weren't even there.

Yeah, just like you saw a cool, handsome guy with a heart in your ex-fiancé, Jonathan, only to realize he was a real toad, not a prince.

What she had was a vision. The power of suggestion. A powerful imagination.

"But I don't get it," Febe said. "Why haven't they, Madam Techer and her sister and butler, you know, moved on?"

Aunt Eartha and Aunt Trixie exchanged glances. "Well, you see dear," Aunt Eartha said in a soothing voice, "they haven't been able to because the people who torched their home when they were in it are still here."

"What? But how? That was almost a hundred years ago!"

"It's a long story, darling. We'll not get into that right now. But rumors had circulated back then that Madam Techer was a witch and her sister, too."

"But what about their poor butler?"

"Oh, that's something we'll talk about another time, darling. He was just at the wrong place at the wrong time."

"I'd say they all were at the wrong place at the wrong time, wouldn't you?"

"Yes, I guess you could say that," Aunt Eartha said.

"Well dear, you need to go back to your lessons or you'll never be accredited as a witch."

"Oh, please. It's not like she can practice out in the open anyway," Aunt Vanity said.

"But she'll need to be all that she can be."

"This is not about joining the army, Eartha."

"I didn't say it was. Although, she will have many battles to face and having the magical ring will help her to focus her energies and to control and protect her reservoir. Right now, she doesn't hold that protection. Besides, we need her to make up the seven witch circle by next year to fight the evil hunter."

"Oh, right. Of course."

"Guys, it's getting busy out there in the dining room. The staff is wondering why all the Summer sisters suddenly hid away in some secret meeting back here in the office." Janvier stood at the door of the kitchen, her apron with the logo, "Summer Café. We'll Make Your Day!" tied around her waist.

Febe always wondered who on earth thought of that logo for the company. She figured it had to be Aunt Trixie who came up with it.

"Very well, we'll be right out."

"Great. We'll also need to order some sandwiches for the police station. They have a meeting for their community baseball team."

"Oh, that sounds fabulous doesn't it?" Aunt Vanity said.

"You will not be flirting with any officers of the law, Vanity," Trixie warned.

"Who on earth said I'd be flirting with a man in uniform? You know how I feel about them."

"What about them?" Febe asked.

"Oh, she went out with this Navy officer once. He broke her heart when he sailed out of her life."

"Sorry to hear that."

"Don't be. He forgot to tell me he picked up women from every continent he went to." She rolled her eyes. "Never again will I trust a man at sea. They're like the waves, up and down and wash away when the first sign of turbulence hits."

"Okay."

"So you will be going back to your lessons, right?" Aunt Eartha asked, hopefully.

"Well, we were discussing the case." Come to think of it, no wonder Madam Techer wanted to help her find the killer.

"Good. Any ideas on who might have done this?"

"Well, we're still far from the truth. Was Darla killed because she was a gossip or because she was a witch? We still don't know for sure."

Knowing the real motive of Darla's death would make all the difference in the world.

Chapter 19

Commanderio stay!
   Commanderio leave!
   Commanderio stop!

Febe woke up in the middle of the night with a start. Her heartbeat raced in her chest and her neck was all sweaty.

Flying books and flying objects and handbags were coming at her, in the nightmare, from every possible direction, slamming into her and there was no way she could stop them.

No amount of *commanderio* worked. In fact, it got worse. She kicked her feet about under the sheets.

"Do you mind? I'm trying to sleep here," a voice sounded in the darkness of the room. "Can't a cat get any sleep without being kicked?"

"What? Oh, um...oh, no. Sorry, Ebony."

"Hey, no worries. Since when did you start talking in your sleep? You okay?" Ebony sounded concerned but there was a hint of annoyance in her tone.

Febe really didn't mean to kick her little kitty.

"I just had a nightmare, that's all," Febe said.

"That's all?" Ebony yawned. "I think you're possessed."

"Possessed? Am not!"

"Are too."

"No, I'm not."

"Yes, you are."

"Who do you think you are?" Febe was beginning to miss the days when her little feline was just that, a feline. Not a talking cat that spoke back to her whenever she felt like it, saying all sorts of ridiculous things.

Besides, if one of them was possessed, it wouldn't be Febe.

"Listen, let's not go through this tonight, okay?" Ebony said.

"Like you have to get up early in the morning to work at the café and study for your witching licensing exam," Febe shot back.

"Oh, please. I'm watching over you. Isn't that work enough?" Ebony stretched on the bed.

"I need to go back to the scene of the crime," Febe said, pushing the covers off her.

"Are you crazy, girl? It's two o'clock in the morning."

"And it's supposed to rain first thing at sunrise which could destroy some evidence."

"Evidence?"

"Yes, evidence. I just thought of something."

"Shouldn't you be telling this to that hot cop you keep drooling over."

"Hey. I do not drool over Detective Trey," she protested, feeling heat climb to her cheeks. How on earth did Ebony even know she had a hint of attraction to him?

"Who said anything about Detective Trey?"

"Isn't that whom you were talking about?"

"No," Ebony gave her a sly grin and arched her brow.

Ebony was up to her tricks again. Playing games with Febe's head. Ever since she could talk, she'd been saying all sorts of stuff to get a reaction out of Febe.

"Besides," Febe said, swallowing a lump in her throat. "Magical folks and normal folks aren't supposed to mix, remember?"

"Oh, right. That's one of the unwritten rules for witches."

"Why is that anyway?" Febe asked, hoping Ebony would have the answers. It was too late to wake up her aunties to ask them.

Ebony yawned again as if she was bored of this conversation. "Isn't it obvious?"

"What's obvious?"

"Oh, come now, for one thing if you married a normal and he found out you were a witch, your very existence would be in jeopardy. Even if he casually mentioned it in conversation somewhere, you could end up being a serious target for witch hunters, a danger he might not be aware of."

"Oh, right," Febe said, suddenly feeling down. Not that she was interested in Trey Heart. Besides, the guy had an attitude. He treated her as if *she* was under investigation or something.

"Then there's the compatibility issues. Heck, normals can't seem to get along with each other. Could you imagine a magical person and normal person in a relationship?"

"Got a point," Febe sighed.

She always felt a world away from her ex-fiancé, whom she wouldn't call normal. Or was he? Maybe he was just a typical guy that liked to fool around on the side.

Still, if she were honest with herself, she had to admit now that they were opposites in lots of things.

He was extrovert, she was more introvert. He liked the wild life and she liked to keep things calm. He was power hungry and she was always...well, hungry. He was thin and well-built and she had a few curves, to put it mildly. He'd always criticized her hips and how she should try to lose weight like paper-thin cut-out Amanda Harlington, their boss, who now she knew, was his secret lover, too.

Oh, well.

"Well, I wasn't drooling over him. He just looked...more like a model than a cop when I first met him, that's all."

"Yeah, right. Remember, I was in the SUV that night when you ran over the body and the cops came to the scene."

"We didn't run over Darla's body! We sort of stumbled on her while driving."

"Keep telling yourself that. I don't know how your sister got her license."

"To drive?"

"To drive and to practice magic."

"You're a bit moody tonight, Ebony."

"Have you ever tried to deprive a cat of sleep? Where do you think the term cat nap comes from? Never deprive a cat of sleep. All cats need between twelve and twenty hours of sleep a day."

"*You* need *twenty-four* hours it would seem."

"Hey, are we getting catty here?"

"Catty? Using those terms, are we?"

Ebony hissed playfully. At least Febe interpreted it as playful.

"I know, I know. It's in your evolutionary genes. In the wild, cats had to hunt in order to eat, and the stalking, chasing, and killing of prey used up a whole lot of energy."

"My dear, Febe, sleeping helps us to conserve energy between meals."

"Hmm-mmm."

"Something that you should be doing more of."

"Sleeping or meals?"

"Both."

Febe frowned.

"Sorry to switch back to the subject of magical folks not mixing with normal folks, but what about Aunt Trixie? She's had a lot of husbands. They weren't all magical, were they?"

"That is something you'll have to take up with your aunt, darling."

Febe reached over to the night table and took up her iPad which had been recharging. Much like she should have been doing while sleeping. Ebony was right. She really needed to get more sleep.

"What are you doing, Febe?"

"Just searching up some recent articles from the Gosnik News website."

"Why? Looking for a bit of juicy gossip to help you fall asleep?"

"Don't be sassy." Who would have ever thought that her kitty would be answering back to her like that?

"I'm sure Darla must have run over someone's nerves in one of her exposés. Madam Techer said she slandered her family's name, too. But what strikes me as odd is that Madam Techer's been dead for what, a hundred years."

"Ninety-seven to be exact," Ebony corrected Febe then let out a nice wide yawn. Febe felt guilty for keeping her feline friend up, but she was obsessed with solving this puzzle. This murder. There was a killer on the loose. She didn't feel one bit comfortable in the town of Blackshore Bay, and neither should anyone else.

Febe opened up her web browser and began to search on Google for the latest articles on the Gosnik News website.

Ebony dutifully climbed over to where she was sitting and snuggled beside her. Suddenly, Febe felt warm and appreciative of having her kitty beside her again. Just like the old days, except now Ebony would answer back to her if she ever stepped out of line.

"Okay, now, let's see what we've got. My instincts tell me that she must have struck a nerve recently with her news articles and somebody exacted revenge on her."

"That's a hunch, is it?"

"Yep. Remember, I've studied human behaviour."

"Oh, right. That nice useless degree you have."

"Hey, it is not useless."

"In the competitive job market it is. Did you really want to get into advertising?"

"You're right, I wanted to be a behavioral scientist conducting studies, but..."

"Yeah, I know. Those two available positions in the country had already been filled," Ebony yawned.

Febe playfully rolled her eyes. "Whatever. You can make fun of my degree but having a speciality in behavioural sciences is, quite to the contrary, a very marketable skill. I can apply that to just about any job in the universe."

"If you say so."

"What would you know about that, anyway?"

"Are you trying to say that I'm just a cat?" Ebony appeared to have raised a brow, which made her look positively adorable.

If only Febe could stop what she was doing and reach for her cell phone to take a snapshot. She could post it to social media and get tons of likes for that.

"No, I'm not saying you're just a cat. You are just a bit much sometimes, that's all."

"Hmmm. Whatever," she purred and rested her chin on Ebony's leg.

"Oh, wait, what have we here?"

Febe scrolled down some of the attention grabbing headlines of the web page. It really was a tabloid style gossip site.

Crazy Cat Lady Chooses Cats over Men

Febe cringed at that title. She knew if she clicked on the hyperlink to the article it would lead to that scandalous piece Darla did on her Aunt Trixie. Her auntie might have a colourful, eclectic personality, but she did not deserve to be slandered like that.

She gave in to the urge and clicked on the link. She read a few passages of the article to see if she could find anything that would have led the police to suspect her auntie and keep her under watch. Even though it was probably obvious from the title alone. Aunt Trixie did not like to be referred to as a cat lady.

She's done it again. Trixie Summer, co-owner of Summer Café has married husband number 7 in a lavish ceremony worthy of the front page. And once again her marriage ended in her husband missing. That's seven missing husbands! Should the police be investigating this lady?

There was an image of Aunt Trixie wearing a lavish, over-the-top massive hat and a long purple gown with beau number seven.

"Aunt Trixie married seven times? I thought it was three."

"Like that would make a difference," Ebony said with another yawn.

Febe started to yawn, too.

"You're obviously tired, now let's go to bed."

"I'm yawning because it's infectious Ebony, not because I'm tired." Which was true. Her energy was pumped now because of the adrenalin rush from the shocking news. "Why am I the last to know about what's going on in the family?"

"Join the club, girl."

"Aunt Trixie really did have an over-the-top ceremony. Is that an elephant in the background?"

"You know your dear old auntie likes to be different, right? It was her fault for enticing the media into her life in the first place. The Summer Sisters used to be in the circus back in the early days. The Sixties, I believe."

"Oh, right. Grandma Summers was a performer in the circus."

"That's right. She used her magical gifts in performance."

Febe remembered her lesson from Madam Techer about some witches choosing to use their gifts in performance, while others branched out to medicine, law enforcement or science. Well, her gifts were using what she knew about human interaction and trying to solve problems. In this case, solve a murder.

"Is there anything else I should know about the family?"

"Not much, except your auntie really knew how to pick 'em."

"Pick what?"

"Losers."

"That's not very kind of you."

"What else would you call gold diggers?"

"Were they all gold diggers?"

"Miss Darla Gosnik, if you read further down, used to publish a cheaters column and would often feature each one of your aunt's lovers, among others in the country, who were caught with an empty ring finger and a lover in a sleazy bar. That's probably why your aunt was all too happy to send them packing."

"So she should be thankful that Darla revealed that."

"Nobody likes the bearer of bad news. That's why they always say don't shoot the messenger. Still, Darla was a little two-faced and would turn around and accuse Trixie of loving her cats more."

"Why does Aunt Trixie have so many cats?"

"Hey, we're cool to be around. Well, most of us anyway. I tried hanging out over at her house once. I won't be doing that again."

"Why?"

"Catty, my dear. Very catty. Anyway, I'm glad she sent me to hang around you and watch over you until you come of age."

"Thanks."

"You sound sarcastic."

"Am not. Just..." Febe paused for a moment.

Cheaters: Who's Doing Who This Week

Cheaters: Submit Your Story if You've been Cheated On

Febe rolled her eyes and scrolled down the web page. "I'm sure she must have had a lot of slander suits."

"She had more suits than the House of Armani warehouse."

"I'm not surprised. Not too many people would care for this sort of stuff."

"She got a lot of revenue from big investors."

Febe frowned.

"What is it, girl? You look discouraged."

"I am. Wouldn't you be? We're just further from the truth." Febe sighed. "Maybe we'll never know who killed her because it could be anyone. Her investors, the guys featured in her Cheaters column, the people in the town…"

"Focus, girl. Isn't that what Madam Techer taught you."

"Yeah. Focus. But where? That's the trouble." She glanced at a few more tabloid headlines with hyperlinks. But didn't bother click on the links. She could not believe the amount of trashing Darla did on that site. She certainly wouldn't have a shortage of enemies.

Crazy Tycoon Going Senile
Crazy Cops Running the Town
Crazy House on the Hill: The Techer Women Still Haunt the Mansion
Crazy Happenings at Town Hall

"You said you saw something at the scene?"

"Yeah, some strange bike marks."

"How do you know?"

"I ride, that's how."

"Well, let's go at five in the morning. That way it's early in the morning before the rain's scheduled to fall."

"Thanks, Ebony. I'm going to take a few snapshots and send them to the police station to look at."

"I hope they appreciate what you're doing. It would be much easier to just send them there."

"But I just want to be sure."

"Sure of what?"

"That I'm right before I send them on a wild goose chase."

Chapter 20

At five o'clock in the morning, Febe got up again after getting two more hours of sleep. She had a quick shower and pulled her hair up into a ponytail.

She grabbed her bike and placed Ebony in her basket.

"What are you doing up this early?" Janvier asked, yawning.

"I thought you'd be at the café already." Febe said, surprised to see her sister.

The house was so massive and Janvier's room was on the other side. She didn't want to risk waking anyone else up in the house, lest they thought she was crazy for what she was about to do.

"I'm heading in when they open. Bud's opening this morning."

"Oh, right."

"What's up?"

"I'm going back to the scene of the...murder."

"What? Why? Are you insane?"

"Janvier, there's a cold-blooded murderer loose and what disturbs me is that no one seems to care because the victim was the town gossip."

"Correction, the victim was the most notorious slanderer this side of the galaxy who used her website to spread malicious rumors about everyone and anyone she could for a price. Did you see that massive piece of real estate she recently bought on the west side?"

"Oh, right. I saw a picture of a mansion on the lake on another site. She bought that recently?"

"Yup. I guess she thought crime paid."

"She didn't commit a crime, did she?"

"She broke a few rules in the witching world. She should have known better than to use her words to harm others."

"Isn't that something?"

"What?"

"People always paint witches as evil women going around uttering curses when in fact, it's against our principles."

"You can say that again."

Febe sighed deeply. "Still, no one deserved to be murdered, not even the town gossip who became an Internet sensation with her gossip news site."

"That site got more hits than a Grammy-winning rock star."

"I guess it did."

"So what are you looking for anyway?"

"A reason to strike up a conversation with that hot cop," Ebony purred.

"Ebony!" Gosh, she wished her cat would hold her tongue once in a while.

"Sorry, just couldn't resist."

"Besides, I'm not interested in men right now. I've had my share of heartbreak and embarrassment, thank you very much."

Ebony rolled her beautiful, large cat eyes.

Janvier just grinned and took a sip of her coffee. "Wait a minute, Sis. Let me get ready. I'm coming with you."

"You don't have to, Janvier."

"Are you kidding me? It's five in the morning. Do you know how dangerous it can be out there in the dark? The sun's not even up yet and you don't have advanced magic like I do."

"I thought you're not supposed to be using magic casually."

"If the situation calls for it, I can. Like if we happen to get into any danger."

"Oh, right. Danger."

Febe realized that she was more vulnerable than she wanted to admit. She didn't have any magical powers that she could control at will. It was probably best that her annoying older sister tag along.

* * *

"So what are we looking for?" Janvier asked an hour later as they walked in the wooded area by the roadside where they had driven over the body the other night.

The sun was beginning to peek through the trees. They knew it wouldn't last long – the area above them had dark clouds moving slowly in the sky.

"Bike tracks."

"Bike tracks?"

"Yup. I thought it was odd that there were tire tracks around the area because it had rained the night before we got here, but I noticed a bike track going along here down the side of the road." Febe glanced at the area. "There's only one track along this path here."

"A motorcycle."

"Right."

"So what, sis? Really now, do you think it had something to do with Darla's death?"

"Possibly."

Just then the girls heard the sound of a twig snapping in the distance. They both froze. Through the trees they saw a shadow of a man.

"I knew it was a bad idea to come out here," Janvier whispered.

"Shh," Febe said, her heartbeat pounding in her throat.

The figure moved closer to the girls at a rapid pace. Febe made a move for it and started in the other direction, pulling Janvier with her. "Please tell me you can use magic to get us out of here," Febe whispered breathless.

"Sorry Sis, it doesn't quite work that way. If it did, Darla would be alive, right?"

"What?" Well that really sucked. What good was using magic if you could only use it in certain circumstances? Her sister had a point though. If Darla was a fully matured witch then she should have been able to save her own life or at least know that impending danger loomed. Sheesh! Power was truly overrated.

"Only the goddess has all full power of everything, Sis. Not us mere..."

"Stop right there!" The man's voice was forceful. "What are you two doing on my property?"

They both turned around. How in Sam's name did he manage to catch up with them so fast?"

"Mr. Calahan." Janvier recognized the man.

"Mr. Calahan?" Febe repeated.

"Janvier Summer? What are you doing here?" He held onto a shotgun and he wore a plaid thick shirt and jeans and mud boots. He also wore a hunter's hat, if one could call it that.

"Um, we were just going for a walk."

"Out here?" He glanced at her dubiously then cast a suspicious eye to Febe.

"Hi, I'm Febe Summer."

He said nothing for a moment. "Cal Calahan."

Okay, was anyone going to tell her who Cal Calahan was?

"You still haven't answered my question," he said.

"Oh, we were just walking."

"You live out here?" Febe asked.

"I live in a cottage not far from here. Use to live in the town but since I got voted off the council I just keep to myself."

"You got voted off the council?"

"Yeah, it's a long story. I'm sure your sister will tell you. Some stupid scandal that I got blamed for. It wasn't my fault. Anyway, I just keep to myself these days."

"How's Mrs. Calahan?" Janvier asked.

"She's okay." His voice was rough and coarse and he started to cough. It sounded like a smoker's cough. If Febe had X-ray vision she wouldn't be surprised if she saw emphysema in his lungs.

Febe's head started to throb. She was getting a massive headache. Maybe it was being in the woods too long, standing in one place. If she could remember correctly, she was allergic to one of the birch trees.

"You were out riding your bike at night I see," Janvier said pointing to the single tire marks.

"So what of it?"

"Oh, nothing. It's just that."

"Are you ladies here about that woman?"

"What woman?" Janvier said, feigning innocence.

"That gossiping hag. I'm glad someone taught her a lesson for spreading lies and ruining marriages on her website. If it wasn't for her, I'd still be on the council."

"Oh, no. I'm sorry to hear that..." Febe took a closer look at Cal and was stunned. She realized where she recognized him from. He'd been featured on Darla's Cheaters section of her news blog. There was a site where readers uploaded pics of known married men going to sleazy clubs and doing all sorts of shady things with scantily dressed women.

Alarm bells went off in her mind.

This didn't look good at all. She couldn't wait to get out of there and tell Janvier about her findings.

"Her website. Everyone knows about that ridiculous tabloid junk."

"Oh, right. I've um...heard about it," Febe said, trying to sound nonchalant.

"Well, I'm glad someone choked the life out of that sinful woman. Good for her. Now that newspaper can rest in peace like her. Shame what she did to her folks' good newspaper."

"Right, of course. But it's still so sad that she...um...was you know, *murdered*!"

"Ha! Good riddance to her."

Febe couldn't believe how cold this man was. "Aren't you afraid that a cold blooded killer is on the loose? They didn't make any arrests yet."

"Course they did."

"They did?" The sisters said in unison.

"Yeah. Sure. It was that fella, that street performer who sings outside the café."

"What?"

Febe couldn't contain herself. "That's preposterous. Yella?"

"Yeah, that's it. Yella. What a fine fella. Hope he gets an award for that."

"Yeah, he'll get an award all right. Fifteen to life!" Janvier said.

* * *

Thirty minutes later, Febe hurried back into the house and dropped off Ebony while Janvier waited in the car. "Now you stay here, sweetie. I'm going to the café, and then I'm going to have a word with Detective Trey."

"You sure you know what you're doing?" Ebony said.

"Of course I do. I may not have much, but my suspicions are right about this. Whenever I get severe headaches, it means something's wrong. Seriously wrong."

"Yeah, something's wrong all right." Ebony then swayed her tail as she strutted across the hardwood floor into the living room.

Febe grabbed her handbag and went outside.

"What time are we supposed to be at the college dorm?"

"At lunch to deliver the Halloween cookies."

"Right. Let's go there, but I'll need to speak with Detective Trey, too. I'm just going to send him a text message. He gave me his card."

"Febe!"

"What? I need to share my thoughts with him about Yella. You don't really think he did it, do you?"

Janvier shrugged. "Sometimes we just have to trust that justice will be done."

Chapter 21

An hour later, Febe stood in the kitchen sticking toothpicks with decorative images of pumpkins and cartoon characters into the Halloween cookies and cupcakes. The college nearby requested the Halloween treats for their fundraiser.

"Darling, there's someone here to see you," Aunt Trixie called out.

Just then the double swinging doors opened and in walked the gorgeous Detective Trey.

"Ms. Summer, you wanted to speak with me," he said, arching his brow.

"Yes, I did," she said, wiping her hands on her apron. "I'll be right with you."

"Take your time."

"What are you doing?" Kris, the baker, said. Kris was a normal, non-magical person. She didn't know that the café was owned by witches.

"I've finished decorating the Halloween treats?"

"With Disney characters? Those aren't scary witches."

"What do you mean?"

"The college wanted scary. You know witches with ugly wart noses, tall hats, creepy looking..."

Febe gave her a you're-not-serious look. "What makes you think witches are really like that?"

"Excuse me?" Kris said, shocked

Febe's heart raced.

Crap.

She'd almost forgotten her place; no one was supposed to know about her...background. Not amongst the normals anyway.

She caught Detective Trey looking at her funny, too, out of the corner of her eye. What must he think of her?

"Um, never mind. I..." she remembered what her aunts said about negative stereotypes about witches. "Listen, let's just deliver these and see what they say. I'm sure they'll like it. It'll be a nice change, right?"

Kris frowned then looked at the large wall clock in the kitchen, "Fine then," she said. "We don't have much time to waste. You need to deliver these by noon."

Febe smiled appreciatively.

Now to the next task.

"So what were you so desperate to speak to me about?" Detective Trey said as he followed Febe out to her sister's SUV. "Do you need help with those?"

"Oh, no. I'm good, thanks." Truth be told, if she were allowed to practice magic, she'd try a witching spell to have the goodies in the vehicle with the twitch of her finger. Never mind that. She'd just concentrate her energies and have it appear at the dorm so that she could get on to finding out what happened to poor Darla.

If only...

Febe opened the door and placed the box of cookies and cupcakes in the back seat. "I'm just on my way over to the dorm up on Main Street. But I heard that you arrested our street performer guy, Yella, for the crime of killing Darla."

"Yes, he was arrested. He's out on bail now."

"Why do you think he did it?"

"We can't go into every detail now, but there were witnesses that corroborated the story that he made threats to Darla when she came by the café. She'd apparently given him a scathing review on her website and said something about him cleaning up the streets by getting off it or something. It's published in the papers."

"Oh, no. But people say all sorts of things, Trey."

"Febe, this is a police investigation. Wait a minute, why am I even telling you all this?"

"We seem to have some sort of connection," she teased.

The truth was, they did seem to gel magically, but she was reminded that now that she knew she was a witch, getting together with a normal was not going to happen anytime soon. Not that she thought about getting together with Trey.

"He said he didn't do it, but we have to follow procedures."

"Who led you to him?"

"Do you know something, Febe? If you do, you should share it with us."

"Not yet. I don't know why I'm even telling you this, but...I just have a feeling that he's being used as a scapegoat while the real killer gets away."

"As far as I know Febe, we've got our guy."

"Let me guess, he didn't have an airtight alibi?"

"He didn't have *any* alibi and he was casual about it, too."

"Hmmm," Febe said thinking out loud. "I think I'm going to pay another visit to Amy at the papers."

"Why?"

"Oh, nothing. Yella isn't the only person she maligned in her reviews."

"Febe, I don't want you snooping around on this case. It's way too dangerous. If the killer is loose out there, your life could be in danger."

Moments later, Trey received another call on his phone and said, "I've got to get back to the station. Remember to let me know if you hear anything, all right?"

"I will."

Febe thought about it for a moment. Maybe she should just keep out of it. But if there was a killer on the loose who was after witches, she really needed to help the cops in the investigation. They'd thank her later. At least she hoped they would.

Chapter 22

Later in the afternoon, after Febe delivered her cookies, she turned up outside the headquarters of the Gosnik News. She sucked in a deep breath, remembering what Detective Trey said earlier. She didn't want to interfere with their investigation, but she didn't want to jeopardize the lives of the witches in her family or the other witches in the town.

What was a witch to do?

"Hey, Febe. You're back," Amy said, greeting her in the reception area.

"Yes, please forgive me, I just need to ask you a few more questions."

"Sure. Come this way."

Febe followed Amy into her office.

"So you've heard about Yella."

"Yes, I did. I don't think he had anything to do with it though. I can't believe they arrested him."

"You think he's innocent, too?"

"Of course. Amy, can I see that article that your sister circled?"

"The one about Florida?"

"Yes, that's the one. I have a feeling we might find a clue in there. There was a diamond-shaped symbol over the state of Florida and a few dollar signs. What does that mean?"

Amy shrugged. "She was always into buying real estate."

"Real estate?"

"Yeah, nice mansions on the lake, like the one she had here. She went to Florida a few times though."

"The Hearts are from Florida, aren't they?"

"Sure, so what?"

"Oh, nothing. I'm wondering if Sergeant Will Heart would know something. Or if he's seen her before. I think it's quite a coincidence."

"You don't think he has something to do with…"

"Oh, no. Not at all. I just think they might know something else."

"Like what?"

"I'm not sure, yet. But I'm going to look over this article if you don't mind. I think your sister might have placed a puzzle inside it."

"A puzzle? Why would she do that?"

"Because she probably knew her killer was after her."

Chapter 23

An hour later, as Febe drove up to the house, her cell phone rang. She pulled over and glanced at the display. It was Trey Heart.

What a sweet name, she thought to herself.

Even his name sounded charming.

Okay, stop that now Febe. You've sworn off men, remember?

"Hello," she answered professionally.

"Hey, Febe. It's Trey."

"Hey, Trey."

"Listen, I did what you asked and I checked out some of the other suspects. I also went back to the area where the body was found. You're right. There was another bike track. Can't seem to place the make. Based on the tire marks it looks as if some sort of foreign ride."

"Foreign, huh?"

"Yes, as in one that's not even made any more."

Febe thought for a moment. "Okay, Trey. Thanks a lot. I think I know what I'm looking for now. I know a few collectors."

"You do?"

"Yes, at the Frutenac Comic Store in Toronto. This guy's really good. He collects and sells rare comics and other stuff."

"Please be careful Febe. I don't want you getting hurt."

"Oh, I will, Trey. Trust me. I don't want to get hurt again either."

"Again?"

"Oh, it's nothing." The last thing she wanted to do was get Trey involved in her pitiful love life or lack of right now.

Febe glanced at her watch. Time was running out. She had hours to piece this puzzle together before the real killer struck again or got away.

Chapter 24

The next day, after her lesson with Madam Techer, Febe sat in the study alone.

"You sure you know what you're doing, girl?" Ebony asked, as she stretched out on her kitty bed.

"I hope so. I need to do this, Ebony. I need to find out what happened to Darla Gosnik. Madam Techer says it's all right to practice at home."

"But you're trying to solve a crime outside the home."

"I know," Febe said, biting down on her lower lip. "She also says I should follow my heart."

"Yeah, not follow Heart."

"Hey. I am not into that guy."

"Yeah, sure. Keep telling yourself that."

Febe tried to focus her attention back on the candle she'd lit in the middle of the study on the coffee table. She glanced at her spell book and took in a deep breath. "Okay here goes...*forces of good, bring to light whatever was hidden in the night*..." she breathed.

Nothing happened.

Ebony yawned and gave her a look.

"Okay, I need to get used to this."

"Are you sure you know what you're doing?"

"Yes. I think I'm closer to solving this mystery. Last night, I had a dream that I met a woman in a long flowing vintage gown—I'm not sure of the era. Sort of like a Victorian era dress. It was weird. Then I saw Darla Gosnik. She too was in a vintage gown. I know it has something to do with the murder. My head just kept pounding like a bass drum last night."

"You're telling me. You were kicking me again."

"Was not."

"Was too. She who feels it knows it."

"Fine. I'm very sorry then."

"Carry on."

A second later, the table collapsed. The wooden legs popped off.

"Ooops. That wasn't the result I was expecting."

"No magic, huh?" Ebony teased, not making it any easier.

Just then Febe's phone rang.

"Who is it?" Ebony asked.

"Oh, it's Amanda Harlington. My former boss." Febe's head pounded, her heart ached in her chest thinking of Amanda with her now ex-fiancé, Jonathan, cheating on her.

She sighed deeply.

"No. Way. What does *she* want?" Ebony asked with a surge of energy.

"That's what I want to know."

* * *

Moments later, Febe got off the phone and sighed heavily.

"So? What did that evil chick want?" Ebony asked.

"She told me that I was right about Jonathan."

"What?"

"Yep. She said she saw him featured in the Cheaters column from the Gosnik website."

"Oh, crap."

"Exactly."

"So she just called you to tell you that?"

"Sort of."

"Didn't she know that once a cheater, always a cheater? I mean what is with humans? If a person cheats on their lover to be with you, what makes you think he won't turn around and do the same thing to you? Sheesh."

"Tell me about it."

"What else did she say?"

"She wants to meet with me for a late lunch tomorrow, around three o'clock. She's going to be in town."

"What? Why?"

"That's what I'm about to find out."

* * *

"You were right," Amanda said the next day at the Summer Café, dabbing her eyes with tissues. "Jonathan is a creep. I'm so sorry. I had to tell you in person. My conscience was killing me."

Febe glanced at Amanda's huge diamond.

"Amanda, you really didn't have to come here to tell me this."

Febe had decided to take a break to see Amanda, so it wasn't officially a lunch. The café was busy, but she explained to Janvier that she wanted to hear Amanda out.

Was Amanda planning on offering Febe her old job back? Would Febe even take it?

"We women have to stick together," Amanda continued, tearfully, "I want you to come back to Harlington Advertising and work your magic for us."

Febe's pulse pounded.

Magic?

Work my magic for them? Did they know about me?

"Amanda. I'm happy here now," Febe said. And even if she wasn't happy there, she had her pride. "What happened?" She tried to be empathetic. But this situation was just plain...pathetic.

"He found someone more powerful than me. My aunt who heads the entire division."

"Oh no." Febe's stomach tightened. Jonathan clearly had no scruples.

"Well, you were right. Please come back and work for us. I'm very sorry."

"I don't know what to say, Amanda. Like I said before, I'm happy here."

Just then Janvier called out from the back.

"I'm sorry, Amanda, but it's getting busy here. I have to get going to take some orders."

Amanda looked disappointed. "Okay. I tried."

She tried? Just what *was* Miss Young and Hot Amanda Harlington up to?

Chapter 25

Later that evening, Febe spoke to Janvier about her conversation with Amanda. They weren't able to talk at the café since it was crazy busy with the tourists and a convention in town. They were both sitting on the couch, glancing over some more information that would help out with the case.

"I can't believe you saw that woman after what she did to you. I thought I got rid of that weak, apologetic sister. Where's the lioness witch in you?"

"I know, I know. She just wanted to apologize in person."

"Yeah, whatever. We don't have time for that. We need to find out who killed Gosnik. Did you check all the links on the top stories for a lead on the murder investigation?"

"Yup. Except this one. Tycoon going crazy. Some senile guy. Rambling..."

Janvier looked it over.

"So you have nothing then."

"Wait." Febe read a passage. "According to the information I gathered at the newspaper, Darla visited a man in Florida who owns an international ad agency. She said he was going senile."

"So?"

Then Febe remembered her lesson from Madam Techer, "Nothing is a coincidence, darling Sis," she said.

"What's that supposed to mean?"

Febe narrowed her eyes and glanced at the screen. "Amanda wasn't here by chance, was she? So what if Jonathan cheated on her?"

"What was Amanda really doing in Blackshore Bay and why?" Janvier added.

Chapter 26

Febe read over the article on the screen.

"In St. Augustine, the oldest city in the U.S., there are reports of a fountain of youth that Ponce de Leon discovered in 1513 soon after he arrived in what we now call Florida."

"Really?" Janvier said. "You know I always thought that was a myth."

"Me too, until now," Febe said, as she continued to read the article. "The city of St. Augustine, Florida is home to the Fountain of Youth Archaeological Park, a tribute to the spot where Ponce de León landed."

"Legend holds that a discovery was made while searching for the Fountain of Youth, a magical water source supposedly capable of reversing the aging process and curing sickness," Janvier read over Febe's shoulders. Her eyes widened in shock.

"Unbelievable," Febe said as she continued to read out loud. "The Fountain of Youth restores youth to anyone who drinks or bathes in its waters."

"Can you believe this?"

"I don't know what to believe Sis," Febe said. She read more from the screen.

"So what do you make of this? Is there a connection?" Janvier asked.

"I think I have the answer."

"You do?"

"I know who killed Darla Gosnik and I think I know why?"

Chapter 27

Moments later, Febe called Amanda on her cell phone, hoping she'd still be in Blackshore Bay.

"Febe, I'm surprised to hear from you again."

"I know what I said earlier but...Let's meet. I think I may consider going back to my old job." Febe crossed her fingers and whispered an apology to the universe for telling this little untruth which wasn't really an untruth. She didn't say she would go back to her old job, just that she'd consider it—sort of.

"Where do you want us to meet?"

"How about the dock near Main."

"Oh, great. My grandfather owns a yacht there. We have property in the area, you know. Cottage country."

Of course you do. "Sounds great," Febe said.

* * *

Later that evening, Febe and Amanda met at the Blackshore Bay dock where the boats were situated. It was a lovely piece of property right on the lake.

"My grandfather used to bring me here when I was little," Amanda said as the waves rocked the boat tied to the dock.

"You mean, you use to bring him here when *he* was little," Febe said, arching her brow. Her heart knocked against her chest at rapid speed.

"Excuse me?"

"Amanda, it took me a while to put two and two together. I spoke with Jonathan."

"That snake. What did he tell you?"

"That you pursued *him*. Because you wanted to suck the energy out of him to thrive in the business. That's what you do."

"Are you insane?"

"Not all the time."

"What?"

"Darla dug up some dirt on your grandfather. He was running into some trouble financially but when she went snooping around his estate, what she found was more valuable. It was the necklace symbol that you have. It's from St. Augustine Florida. I thought about what kind of possible connection there could be. What would be so damning that would make Darla see dollar signs? The Fountain of Youth."

"The what?"

"You know. Don't play dumb. The Fountain of Youth was located in Florida back in the 1500s. It was where the explorer came seeking it and founded the first city in the US. You drank from that fountain, but there was a catch. You had to suck the life out of every viable creature and you thought Jonathan was vibrant until you realized that it was my ideas that he stole. You would have loved to suck the creative energy out of me."

"Well, aren't you a clever girl. How on earth did you figure it out?"

"It wasn't easy, but as you know, or should have realized from my resume, I have impeccable research skills," Febe said. *And a witch's badass intuition.* "Tedious details are my OCD thing. I never stopped looking until I found what I was looking for and pieced the puzzle together. Your grandfather is really your *son*!"

"What?" Amanda's eyes widened in shock.

"I remember overhearing your phone conversations with him at the office. I was appalled at the way you spoke to him and treated him like a child and always called him by his first name. I thought it was strange at first, but now it all makes sense. He's not your grandpa, he's your child. How awful for you to see him grow old while you stay the same as you have all these centuries. No wonder I dreamt about a woman wearing a vintage dress. It was you. You drank from the water in the 1500s and never aged. Got married and had a child in 1940, then you taught him everything you knew about the business. Just so that it wouldn't look suspicious, you pretended to be his granddaughter, but in fact he never married or had any children. You just came out of nowhere, hoping your past wouldn't creep up to you, but Darla with her tabloid investigative journalism skills figured it out and was about to publish a massive exposé if you didn't pay up."

"That witchy woman. I'm glad I killed her. But you'll never be able to prove it."

"I wouldn't count on that."

"I figured out that you were a witch," Amanda continued, "I always felt a strange energy force around you. No wonder I couldn't get too close to you. But I still have more than what you could possibly have. I have immortality."

"Dying ain't so bad, Amanda. Living in hell is worse."

"Excuse me?"

"If you had to serve a life sentence in prison for the crimes you committed including murdering Darla Gosnik, I bet your immortality wouldn't seem so hot."

She shrieked. "I'm going to kill you."

"Freeze!" Detective Trey called out.

Seconds later, more cops appeared at the scene.

Everything happened so fast.

"I am not going to prison for eternity!" she shrieked as they took her away. "I'm not going to prison!" Her eyes opened wide and she reached for her neck and ripped off the diamond choker that she wore around it.

She started to wrinkle like Febe had never seen before. Right before their eyes, she became old and grey. It was dark and Febe could tell Trey was just as alarmed as she was.

Amanda then backed away onto the edge of the dock and hurled herself into the water.

She was gone.

Chapter 28

"So the boss from hell was *really* a boss from hell, wasn't she?" Aunt Trixie said later that evening as the women gathered in the grand living room by the fireplace. "Imagine that."

"It looks that way," Febe agreed, "She knew her own son, whom she called her grandfather, wouldn't spill her secret, but she never counted on him talking to a tabloid journalist from the small town with a big scandal-mongering website. Of course this scandal could have sent shockwaves around the world if it ever got out."

"So there really is a fountain of youth, is there?" Aunt Vanity said, fixing her hair and glancing into a mirror. What else was new? "I wish I'd known that, I'd hate to lose my beauty when I reach a hundred."

"You'd lose a whole lot more than that, Sis," Aunt Trixie teased.

"But why on earth would anyone want to live forever? Surely they'd get tired after they reached 200," Febe said.

Janvier grinned. "I'm sure they'd be more worn out before they got to 200. Still, people chase the wrong things and do desperate things."

"Yeah, tell me about it."

"Speaking of chasing," Aunt Vanity said to Febe. "You going to be chasing that hot detective anytime soon?"

"I don't think so," Febe said softly, feeling butterflies in her tummy.

Goodness, was she having a sweet chemistry with this guy? "But he asked me to lunch so..."

"Lunch?" Aunt Vanity's voice was filled with excitement. "Oh, that's wonderful. Maybe you two can date? And get married and..."

"Vanity, you know witches and normals are not supposed to mix," Aunt Eartha said.

Febe frowned.

Why on earth not? Okay, she knew why. But she really had a hard time getting used to that. The one guy that made her heart go pitter-patter, something that she never felt with her ex-fiancé, and she just realized that even after meeting her potential soul mate, they can't, well, mate? How unfair was that?

"I am going to have lunch with him this week, but, I don't think it could go any further," Febe said, regretfully, hoping there was some way they could date.

"And why not? Want me to whip up some love potion?" Aunt Vanity winked.

"You will do no such thing." Aunt Eartha interjected.

"Aunt Eartha, you took the words right out of my mouth," Febe said. "I already told you, I'm on break now. We're just going as friends. And even if we weren't, I don't believe in using love potions. True love is already magical."

"Hear, hear, niece," Aunt Eartha agreed. "True love is magical. You don't need a potion for that."

So was that what Febe was feeling for Trey? A deep love connection?

"Keep telling yourself that niece. I saw the way you looked into his beautiful eyes—and the way he kept looking at you. Why do you think he kept following you around? You think he suspected you? No. He was trying to protect you. He was into you in more ways than one and you were too blind to see it."

"You think that's what he was doing?"

"Of course. I heard him talking to one of his mates down at the café and at the gym. I didn't want to say anything earlier because you were focusing on helping him in the murder investigation. But I heard a lot of nice things he's said about you. I get around, you know."

"I bet you do," Aunt Trixie added.

Aunt Vanity rolled her eyes at her sister. She then turned her attention back to Febe. "Anyway, he *is* gorgeous, isn't he? He works out at the gym a lot too."

Febe tried hard not to blush. Yes, she noticed that too. He had quite a physique. He was so sweet to her earlier, making sure that she was all right.

Of course, she'd called Trey first before meeting Amanda, with the plan to try to get Amanda to confess to the crime so they could make their arrest. He had been reluctant at first worrying about her safety, but got the go-ahead from his department.

The night didn't quite work out the way they'd planned though. With Amanda morphing into an old woman.

Still, he had to fill out a report for his boss, his uncle Sergeant Will Heart. That wasn't easy, but they went with the truth. Well, the part of the truth that was believable. The part where they went to make the arrest but Amanda plunged into the lake. When the coroners found her body, it was so badly wrinkled, they figured it had to be the water pressure or something. They just didn't know what to think.

At least that was taken care of.

Just then a knock sounded at the door.

Febe made her way over to the door to answer it, but a gust of wind met her instead.

"Who is it?" Aunt Eartha called out from the living room.

There was an envelope made of parchment paper on the front porch stuck onto the rocking chair.

She picked up the envelope and opened it.

Better practice your magic spells.
You're going to need them soon.
One by one,
the Summer sisters will soon be gone.

Who sent this letter? Most importantly, how on earth did they know the Summer sisters were witches?

Somebody was watching them closely.

* * *

The story continues in "Life's a Witch" book 2 of the Summer Sisters Witch Cozy Mystery series.

Don't miss the next installment. Sign up for notification at annmarieking.author@gmail.com

* * *

Thank you for reading this installment in *The Summer Sisters Witch Cozy Mystery series.*

Coming soon...

More magical stories set in the cozy small coastal town of Blackshore Bay in *The Summer Sisters Witch Cozy Mystery series.*

The Summer Sisters Witch Cozy Mystery series:

Witch Happens (Book 1)

Life's a Witch (Book 2)

Witch You Were Here (Book 3)

ABOUT THE AUTHOR:

A.M. King enjoys reading and writing cozy mysteries. Join her email list for updates on more cozy mysteries that will make your toes curl and your heart smile. You can send her an email at annmarieking.author@gmail.com with the subject line: **Email Sign-Up**.

She loves to hear from readers.

9 781386 751595